MODERN MAGIC

Enrapturing Tales is an imprint of:

Knight Writing Press
PMB # 162
13009 S. Parker Rd.
Parker CO 80134
knightwritingpress.com
KnightWritingPress@gmail.com

Interior Book Design and eBook Design by Knight Writing Press

Editor Sam Knight

First Publication November 2022

Paperback ISBN-13: 978-1-62869-060-6
eBook ISBN-13: 978-1-62869-059-0

DEDICATED TO YOU. NEVER FORGET:

MORNING CUP OF MODERN MAGIC

SOME MAGIC YOU HAVE TO MAKE YOURSELF

TABLE OF CONTENTS

A NOTE FROM THE EDITOR

I have always felt the world was full of magic. From the magic words I would say in my head when I shot a basketball at the hoop on my grandparent's garage, to the strange things I've seen that I couldn't explain, to the feelings I get when the smells of the holidays fill the house.

How can the smell of cinnamon and cloves make you feel warm, happy, and safe if magic is not involved somehow? How is it the whole world so often goes still and quiet in that golden hour before sunset if there's no magic? How can squiggly lines of black ink on a page in a book make words that can, years later, teach you something, change the way you feel, think, and live, if there is no such thing as magic?

In today's world, magic can seem a little hard to come by. Which is really too bad. I think it probably needs magic more than ever. Even the youngest children seem jaded to the world around them.

As you read our stories of people who found magic, keep in mind the places you once found magic in your life. Maybe you'll remember where, and how, to look for it. Maybe, just by looking, you'll alert the magic to your presence, and it will come looking for you.

But even so, some magic you still have to make for yourself. Don't be afraid to put in a little elbow grease, either, because that's definitely a key ingredient. Right up there with rainbows and shooting stars.

And for sure don't be afraid to try to make magic yourself. Everything starts somewhere. It might as well start with you. Right here, right now, and with this book.

-SAM KNIGHT
OCTOBER 4TH, 2022

BROKEN THINGS

BY
DAMIEN MCKEATING

BROKEN THINGS

There's this trick that I can do; my one true talent. But, I tell you now, it is not quick thinking.

Daisy stomped through the living room, a delirious blur of rainbow-coloured hair, piercings and leather. She sobbed and pounded up the stairs in her big boots. I stood with my mouth open, a mug of tea halfway to it. I couldn't remember if I was going to drink it or say something to her. Something suitably parental like, "Take your boots off," or "What's the matter, love?"

Didn't, though. Just stood there like a hedgehog who's realised he's on a main road.

"Should I?" I half-asked, nodding towards the stairs.

"No," Ellie said. She stood in the kitchen doorway, arms folded across her chest, looking tired.

"Bad one?" I asked.

"She and Jesse broke up."

"Aw, man."

I put the mug down and, in the absence of Daisy, hugged Ellie. We look odd together. I'm tall and broad and quiet, she's short and slim and a firecracker. Somehow, we've always fit together.

"She'll be okay. Give her some time. We all get our heart broken at some point."

"We didn't," I said.

"I was heart-broken when I met you," she said, looking up at me.

"The first thing I fixed," I smiled and kissed her.

"Not quite," she smiled back and slipped away. "I've got to pick up a few things. Are you staying here?"

"Yeah. For a while. I'll hang around, just in case she needs someone." I finished with a shrug.

I watched Ellie leave and thought about how she'd been when we first met, thirty-something years ago. We weren't much different, even then. She was a lean tomboy with scuffed knees and a wicked punch. I was a tubby kid who'd rather be neither seen nor heard.

She was sitting in the dirt, sniffling, wiping at her nose with the back of her hand, a threadbare teddy in two pieces in front of her. Someone had ripped its head off. A little cloud of white stuffing stuck out from the neck.

"Are you okay?" I asked, immediately wanting the sky to fall in and bury me.

"Sam broke my Ted," she said.

"Oh." I shuffled my feet and looked to the horizon for inspiration. "Should we tell someone?"

"No," she sniffed. "I think I broke his nose." She shrugged.

I was in love. I decided to show her the trick that I could do. I'd never shown anyone else. I knew, just knew, that it wasn't something everyone could do, and if they knew I could do it then I would…stand out. I couldn't think of anything worse.

I took hold of the two halves of Ted in my hands. I gently placed the head back onto the neck and covered the join with my palms.

Now, I don't know how it works, not really. Never did, never have done, probably never will. I just know that I can do it. I can *feel* how things should fit together. The stitches and tears in the bear's neck seemed to appear in my mind's eye and then slot together—like a laser light show across the night sky.

I moved my hands away and Ted was whole again.

"You fixed him," she said, stating the obvious only because it was so unbelievable. "How did you do that?"

I shrugged. Embarrassment washed over me. If the sky wasn't going to fall down and crush me, maybe I could dig my way into the ground and bury myself alive.

Ellie hugged me. It was wonderful. She was strong and wiry. I could smell the soil on her skin, the perfume sting of her soap, feel her soft hair against my face, and the breath of her words against my ear.

"Thank you," she said.

It was love and I fell hard. Never had the guts to think she might feel the same. Took me a few more years to figure that out.

Maybe I was still figuring it out. Think maybe that's what love is, really: figuring it out new each day.

From upstairs came the sound of thudding punk rock. Loud and aggressive. Full of fire and life. I'd always liked to drown in music, so I could understand that. When you don't have the words, let someone else sing or scream them for you.

I decided to give Daisy some space. I went out to the garden, easing the pain out of my dodgy leg with each step, hauled open the garage door and set to work.

I fix things. Not just in that special way, but in the everyday kind of way. I think one led to the other. I wanted to know how things went together, so I ended up studying mechanics and engineering. Now I fix pretty much everything. Everyone around town knows who I am and sends me things, and I do a good mail-order business around the country, even a few international orders.

The garage is an orderly mess. There are two long workbenches with the tools arranged and stored just how I want them. Then there are rows, stacks, and boxes of works-in-progress. Years ago, Ellie hit upon the idea of bargain hunting in antique stores, charity shops, auctions, and car boot sales. We were buying the broken stuff cheap, fixing it up, and turning a good profit. So now there were paintings, books, toys, mirrors, and clothes in amongst the usual furniture, machinery and electronics.

I can lose hours at a time when I start working. It draws me in and the world fades away. It's soothing; like a good yoga session, or meditation. I imagine. Never been much good at yoga or meditation, but I've heard people talk about it.

I work with my hands, feeling wood, metal and plastic beneath my fingers. I manipulate the pieces with my flesh and my mind. Each time there's that laser show behind my eyes where the strands of energy, of molecules, knit together. Just like magic. Or chemistry. I can never decide what it is I actually do.

When I stop there's still loud music thudding out of the upstairs room. I message Ellie, tell her I'm going for a walk, and give Daisy some more space. Good thing there are no neighbours nearby for her to annoy; and it also means plenty of space for me to walk. I like to walk. It gives me time to think, and it eases the pain in my leg. After a few miles my limp usually starts to ease up.

We live in an old farmhouse, surrounded by a good stretch of land. The house was a wreck when we found it and optimistically sold as a "fixer-upper." As luck would have it, that kind of thing was no problem for me. We got a dream house for a dream price, and the space and quiet I'd been craving since I was a kid.

Recent storms had kicked up leaves and deadfall across the track from our house. There's a patch of woodland nearby with a dirt track cutting through it, and a main road into town that cuts close to it and then follows the river. It's a thirty-minute walk into town, if you walk like you mean it.

Today I didn't mean it at all. I meandered. I felt the wind on my face, heard the rustle of birds in the branches, and wondered if the greying clouds meant rain.

A tree by the path had lost a branch. I picked it up and felt the rough bark against my rough palms. I turned the branch in my hands and held it up to the trunk of the tree. It was a living thing, not like the materials I usually worked with. I wondered if I could do it. I'd done something like it, once...

Bobby Fenn had fallen out of a tree. We were just daft teenagers, messing around and building a rope swing too high on a branch too weak to support us. Should have known better, but we didn't, and the inevitable happened.

I remember the sounds. Two cracks. The branch and his leg. There was a silence afterwards like the world had ended. I'd have sworn it lasted forever, but then suddenly Bobby was screaming.

I looked at his leg and saw how bad it was. It was...bad. Then Bobby stopped screaming, and that was worse. His face was pale and drenched in sweat. Pain, shock, or something had knocked him out. I sat on the ground next to him, relieved to see that he was still breathing, and wondered what the hell to do.

We were too far from anywhere for me to carry him, or drag him, and neither seemed like a good idea anyway. No one was likely to find us. We were alone. Bobby was probably dying. I vomited and then decided there was only one thing to do.

It's the only time I've ever done it: fixed living matter. I placed my hands on his leg and let the magic flow...

8

I don't remember much about it, truth be told. My jaw snapped shut and I thought my teeth might grind themselves to dust. There was a pain behind my eyes like a nail had been driven through my skull. The lights I saw…lines and patterns, the intricate weft and weave that bound bone to bone and flesh to flesh.

Turns out, somebody did find us. We were both unconscious. I had dried blood over my face from a nosebleed and Bobby had blood all over his leg, but no wound. Not a single trace of his broken leg.

The only thing that changed that day is I now walk with a limp. I guess there's a cost to something like what I can do.

The dull ache in my leg reminded me that I'd stopped walking. I put down the tree branch, letting go of it and the memory of Bobby Fenn. I turned towards home and wondered how Daisy was doing. I wanted to do something. I'd make her pain my own, if I could. I remember nursing her as a kid, every time she was sick, and praying that I could take away everything that was hurting her and carry it myself.

"We all get our heart broken at some point," Ellie's words echoed back to me.

But how do you fix a broken heart?

I stopped.

Like I said, I'm not known for my quick thinking. The idea must have been knocking around in the twilight of my subconscious for hours, but now it had stepped out into the daylight.

I can fix things.

Could I fix a broken heart?

What would it cost me?

Did it matter? I'd do anything for Daisy. I'd bear any pain. I'd die for her, without question or hesitation.

I kicked the idea around as I walked. I could fix small things, things that weren't alive, and it didn't seem to cost me anything. Nothing that I'd noticed, anyway. Sometimes I wondered if a debt was building: maybe there was a cancer growing in me, or I was chipping away at the hours and days of my life. But Bobby's leg had cost me, and a broken heart felt bigger than a broken leg.

The house was quiet when I got home. I lingered outside the garage. The world felt like it was slipping around me, like reality had shaken itself loose. The idea that had taken hold of me was too big: I was sure people could see it radiating off me.

I made my way to Daisy's room and knocked on the door.

"You okay, Day?" I said.

"Yeah," she replied after a while. There was weight in that one word. I could feel the effort it had taken for her to say even that much.

"Get you anything?"

"No. I'm tired."

"Get some sleep, love. I'll be downstairs."

What had I expected to do? To tell her my plan? To just burst in and lay hands on her, like some crazed healer?

I was standing in the kitchen, holding a mug of tea, and gazing out across the garden when Ellie came home, hauling two shopping bags with her.

"Huh?" I said when I realised she was talking to me.

"What's going on?" she asked.

"Oh. Nothing." I sipped my tea, gagged at how cold it was, and put it on the counter.

"Right," Ellie said. "Nothing at all. How's Daisy?" She started unloading the bags and packing things away into the cupboards.

"Said she was tired."

"You spoke to her?"

"Only a little. Did some work. Went for a walk. Been thinking."

"I know."

"You know?"

She smiled. "You've got a thousand-yard stare going on. You look like your brain might melt out of your ears."

I gave a small laugh and felt my cheeks flush a little. "It's a big thought," I admitted.

Something in my tone caught her attention. She stopped what she was doing and took hold of my hands. "What is it?" she asked.

"You said she was heart-broken," I said. I turned my hands over in hers so I was looking down at my palms.

"She is."

"Could I fix her?"

I looked up and locked eyes with Ellie, so I felt the full force of her rage. Her eyes went wide as she turned ashen.

"No."

"Just a thought," I said.

"No," she repeated, bringing a hand up to slap my arm. She stepped away from me, her body rigid with fury. "Did you hit your head when you went walking?"

"No. I was thinking about Bobby and his leg."

"Fixing Bobby's leg almost killed you."

"It's just a limp."

"They found you unconscious, covered in blood, lucky that the bleeding had stopped before your brains oozed out through your nose."

I shuffled my feet and shrugged my shoulders. I hadn't moved, penned into my corner of the kitchen while Ellie stalked the room.

"I don't want anything to hurt her," I said. I clasped my hands and interlocked my fingers. "I can put things back together."

"A broken heart isn't a literal thing." Ellie said. She sighed, her shoulders dropping, her voice quieter. "Even if...even if it was something you could do, how do we know it's a clean break? Does a broken heart feel broken or does it feel shattered?"

"Yeah," I agreed, my chin down on my chest, my voice down in my shoes.

Ellie placed her palms on my chest. "Don't," she said. "Don't even think about it. Some things just have to heal themselves."

"Is it..." I struggled to organise my thoughts, to make sense of something that was unsaid. But I'm not the quickest of thinkers. "I didn't know how important it was. To you."

"Honey, you'd be..." Now she struggled for the words. "You'd be changing someone against their will. Imposing your own ideal onto them. Controlling them."

"No."

"Not cruelly," she said, holding my gaze and stroking my cheek. "But you'd still be manipulating them. And...I couldn't bear that. If you could do it to them, could you do it to me? Love only means anything when it's free."

We held each other. I cried and there was a release in it. A weight I hadn't known was there lifted from my chest. Ellie was right, of course. She'd seen something here that I hadn't. What would be the cost of fixing a broken heart? Maybe not my death, but something more sinister. A loss of something I might never see coming.

"Never," I said, my face nestled into Ellie's hair. "I promise."

There was a sense of space around me as I went out into the garage. Space was what I wanted. I needed to think about what Ellie had said, about how I felt, but the sensation around me was unsettling. The space felt like an absence, as if I had lost something; like the nightmare of realising you don't have your trousers on.

I tried to work but my mind wouldn't focus. There was a painting I wanted to restore: a crack in the frame and a tear in the canvas. Both should have been the work of seconds, a moment under my hands, but I didn't want to do it. I got out my tools and began to glue, fill and sand the frame. There was a solace in the physicality of the work.

What was the cost of my talent?

"Dad?"

Daisy stood in the doorway, looking at me with the same concerned frown Ellie had been wearing. "You okay?" she said.

"Fine. Just working."

"Didn't look like it."

"Thinking too," I said with a shrug. I placed the frame down, satisfied with how it was coming along.

I've never told Daisy what I can do. Only Ellie knows. I don't know what would happen if others found out. I've never wanted to stand out, to feel like a freak, or be exploited, but I had helped people. I hoped I had, at least.

"How are you?" I asked.

"Still tired," she said and put her arms around me.

I hugged her back. There's something special in these moments. You remember when they were tiny and it seems that, no matter the age or size, they've always fit together with you. Like you were meant to be. Bonded. Fixed together.

"I wish I could make it better," I said.

"It'll get better," Daisy said.

"I know it hurts." I kissed her on the forehead. "I'd take it all away, if I could."

"No," she said with a shake of her head and a sardonic half-smile. "It's mine. I'll live through it." She reached into her pocket. "Could you fix something for me?"

My heart jumped. "Sure," I said.

She handed me a silver heart on a chain. The chain had snapped and come away from the pendant. "I don't know how to put it back together."

"I can do that," I said. "This was from Jesse?"

"Yeah," she said with a shrug. "I just… I don't know. I feel like when I'm eighty years old, I'll want something to look back on and think about."

I looked down at the locket nestled in my palm and I chuckled. "You're smarter than me," I said.

"I know." She gestured at the locket and then around the garage. "How do you do it?"

I looked up to see that Ellie had followed us out. She was standing at the doorway and had obviously heard the end of the conversation. She nodded at me.

I swallowed and licked my lips. My heart was racing, and I felt light, as if a strong wind could blow me away.

"I can show you," I said. "There's this trick that I can do."

And I closed my hand around the tiny heart in my palm…

ABOUT THE AUTHOR

Damien has written stories since his primary school teachers taught him how to put letters together into words. If he looks vague when he talks to you, he's either working on another story in his head, or the kids haven't slept again. He is fond of corvids and is currently the oldest he has ever been. Sometimes he remembers to blog.

skeletonbutler.wordpress.com

SPHERE OF FALLING

BY
STACE JOHNSON

SPHERE OF FALLING

It sat in my palm, small, round and shiny. The fluorescent lights of the shop reflected, curved, in its surface, as did the face of the shopkeeper. His nose, already a work of grotesque art, was even more hooked and crooked when viewed in the round surface, and the transparent green visor that shaded his eyes looked even sillier in reflection than in reality.

I had expected the sphere to be cool when he dropped it into my sweaty hand, but it was warm. And it didn't really drop; it sort of settled into my hand, like a bird settling into a nest. I could barely feel its weight.

"And this will cure my…phobia?" I asked the shopkeeper, one eyebrow raised.

"Yessir. Not only will it cure your fear of stairs and ladders, it will keep you from falling no matter what. The Sphere of Falling works for any kind of falling-related phobia. Once you buy a Fear Sphere™ of any kind, you're protected from that fear completely, whether real or imagined. It's guaranteed."

My hand felt light, as if it were floating. I brought the sphere to my face and looked at my oversized nostrils in the reflection. The sphere smelled faintly acrid, like air after a lightning strike. I held it to my ear but heard nothing. No whirring, no high-pitched electrical whine.

"What makes this work?" I asked the shopkeeper.

His lips pursed and quivered for a second before he answered. "I'm not allowed to say. Contractual obligations." He tilted his head toward a crystal ball on the top of his desk. Grey smoke swirled inside the ball; I didn't look too closely, simply nodded.

He squinted out from under his visor. "Let's just say it's not any new-fangled electronic device, hmm?" The visor shifted up on his forehead as he raised his bushy brows and winked once. He pulled the bill back down with his forefinger and thumb. I rolled the sphere around in my palm with my forefinger, looking for manufacturing marks. There were none.

"Why don't you give it a try, eh? There's a ladder just over there." He angled his head toward the end of the counter, where a rollaway ladder leaned against the shelves.

I looked at the ladder, expecting my heart to start pounding, and was surprised when it didn't. I closed my hand over the small silver sphere and placed it gently in my sport coat pocket. Glancing first at the shopkeeper, I walked slowly to the ladder, like a cowboy approaching a skittish horse. The ladder didn't move, and the shopkeeper followed behind me. I licked my dry lips before I spoke.

"You know, I've never really had a problem with heights, but ladders are tricky for me because they aren't too stable. Especially ladders with wheels," I rambled, looking at the cast iron rails on which the ladder rode.

"Then this will be a good test," the shopkeeper said. He sounded confident; I remained unconvinced but took a deep breath and put my right foot on the first step.

The ladder didn't move, and I didn't slip and fall. Holding tight to the ladder's edge, I carefully lifted my left foot up to the step, and again the ladder stayed put. I looked at the shopkeeper.

"Go on," he said, grinning like a proud father.

The second step was as easy as the first, but I had no intention of going higher. I remembered what had happened the last time I climbed that high on a ladder. I still had the scar on my forehead to prove it.

"Okay, it seems to work. I think I'll come down now."

"No sir, you'll keep going right on up to the top of those steps. We have to give the Sphere a good test to make sure it works for you, now don't we?"

I thought about what he said and realized how empty the space behind my fear was. Beyond that one fearful memory, nothing lurked to keep me from climbing higher up the ladder. "Okay," I said.

I steeled myself for the inevitable unbalanced feeling as I brought first one foot, then the other, to the third step, and was pleased to find that the step was solid. The nagging trepidation that had been bothering me since I looked at the ladder began to change into a sense of thrill.

I mentally latched onto that, grabbed the shelves for support, and climbed another step. Still no vertigo, no irresistible urge to jump. I moved up to the fifth step, and still the ground did not reach up to grab me. I looked past my right foot at the old shopkeeper.

"Go on!" he said again, waving his hands upward. "Only one more to go!"

I placed my right foot gingerly on the final step, clinching the shelf brackets for balance. The step creaked a little but took my weight. I slowly moved my other foot up beside it and applied weight until I was completely supported by the top step. My fingers relaxed their grip a little. I felt as if I were standing atop a brick wall, stationary and solid.

"See? There's nothing to it!" the shopkeeper said, spreading his arms.

Then he kicked the ladder out from under me.

The ladder clattered down the rail to the back of the shop, banging into the rubber stopper at the end of the rail and rebounding a few inches. The shopkeeper's grin had changed from fatherly to maniacal. I screamed...but I did not fall. Instead, I floated in mid-air, my fingers white against the surface of the dusty shelves.

"Wha—what the hell'd you do that for?" I shrieked.

The shopkeeper's wild grin retreated into a smile again, comforting and apologetic. "Just helping you test the product. See? It works like a charm... If you'll pardon the expression. You can come on down now, if you want."

"How?" My voice trembled around the word.

"Just tell yourself you want down, and you'll come down, gentle as a feather."

I licked my lips and whispered, "Down, please, now." The shelves seemed to rise in my hands at first, but then I realized I was slowly dropping — not falling — down to the floor. I relaxed my grip and let my hands slide down the worn woodwork. When my feet touched the floor, I took a deep breath. The orb still rested in my pocket, warm and comforting.

"S-Sold," I said, fishing a card out of my wallet. I tapped the card against the reader and entered my PIN. A little brass bell above the door jingled as another customer came in.

"You want to carry that, or should I box it up for you?" the shopkeeper asked.

"I think I'll just carry it, thanks."

"I thought you might." He smiled and winked out at me from under the visor, his face glowing green in the filtered fluorescent light.

As I left, I heard the other customer saying, "I, um… My girlfriend wants to get married…"

"Ah, I have just the thing for you: a Sphere of Commitment. Fix you right up!"

The shopkeeper continued talking as I walked out. The doorbell chimed goodbye, and I floated down the steps to the sidewalk.

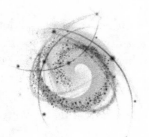

ABOUT THE AUTHOR

Stace Johnson is a writer, musician, and IT professional in Denver, CO. He has more than 100 publications spanning fiction, non-fiction, and poetry, and can be found participating on panels and performing music at several Front Range science fiction conventions.

Learn more at www.lytspeed.com, or visit his writer and musician page on Facebook at facebook.com/Lytspeed

ETERNALLY SHACKLED
BY
STEPHANIE DAICH

ETERNALLY SHACKLED

How can Josephine run a farm alone?" I ask my mom. I shift the phone to my left ear as I gather the grocery bags with my right hand. I use my wide hip to close the car door. Could there be anyone lazier than my hillbilly cousin, Josephine? Whenever we were together as kids and the adults gave us jobs, Josephine instantly developed a stomach malady or a bad case of female cramps.

"Where did you say her farm is?"

My mom's voice sounds muffled. "It's on her property in Arkansas. She used her inheritance money and brought in animals."

I drop the grocery bags at my feet as I fiddle with my keys to open the front door. The phone slips from my ear, and I quickly catch it before it shatters on the porch.

The stiff hinges make it hard to push my apartment door open. I wedge my leg in front of it and scoop up my groceries. I trip on two dogs and three cats as I shove my way into my apartment. My family of pets assault me. Maybe I have a little of the hillbilly gene in me, but nothing like Josephine.

"Hey, babies," I say, shutting the door. These little guys are my family. I don't have time for real relationships.

I adjust the slippery phone, covered in sweat, then continue to balance it under my shoulder. "Who helps her? There is no way Josephine is motivated enough to run a farm."

"She does it by herself," my mom says.

As I make my way to the kitchen, Lady, my golden retriever, jumps on my chest, and my phone flies to the kitchen tile.

Crack.

"Oh no!"

The groceries slip.

Crunch.

"Lady!"

Josephine has a farm. What a strange thought. As I juggle my life with Marcus Wollen, my boss, I think about Josephine's farm. I bet those poor animals are starved and neglected.

"Cathy, I need those files now!" Marcus screams at me with a level two tone. My head bobs up.

I once had categorized the intensity of his screams. Level one—He wanted something, but not urgently. Level two—He was getting desperate but not emergent. Level three—I better respond in three seconds flat or find a new job.

I steady my tone, keeping myself from snapping back. "The printer service said the documents would be ready at 2 p.m. That is still an hour away. I thought I would get your..."

Marcus interrupts me. "I don't need to know what you thought. Go to the printer service and tell them you need the files now!"

As I drive to the printer service, I make several micro stops for Marcus. I have used the printing service for three years. They won't have the files ready until 2 p.m., and arriving earlier would only waste my time, which I never squander—me, queen multi-tasker.

After I pick up Marcus' lunch, I head to the printers. I engage my phone's speech recognition.

"Call Josephine."

"Hey-a-cuz," her southern drawl burst out of my car speakers. "What you up to? Haven't heard from you since the funereal."

"Yeah, sorry about that."

Wait, communication goes both ways. She could have reached out to me anytime over the last two years. In fact, she has more time in her life than I do. I mean, what has she been doing, sitting on her butt? I bite my tongue.

She asks, "You still working for that hotshot legal service?"

"Yes."

"Sounds dull. I don't think I could ever leave the country and move to the city."

"I heard you got a farm."

Josephine's voice raises. "I did, I did! I'm a genuine farmer now."

"How many animals do you have?"

A car swerves into my lane. I slam on my breaks. "Freaking idiot!"

"What?"

"Oh, sorry, not you, Josephine. I am driving."

"Yup, another reason I hate the city. But, to your question, I don't know how many animals I have."

"How do you have a farm and not know how many animals you have?"

"I dunno. Haven't counted, I guess." How can she not know what animals she has? They surely have to be neglected.

The traffic light turns yellow, and I would run it, but a cop pulled up behind me. I slam on my breaks as the light turns red.

Josephine asks, "Ya married yet?"

I stare at the red light. *Turn green already!* "Um, no. I don't have time for marriage. Between my job and my pets, I think I have all I can handle." Linda, my coworker, had tried to get me to do a speed dating activity two weekends ago, but I had to bail when Marcus needed me to run to Hot Springs, Arkansas for him and appease a client. It pissed me off, but I hadn't really wanted to do the dating thing anyways.

Without thinking, I ask, "What about you? Married?" The light turns green, and I make a left-hand turn, almost creaming someone. I hope the cop didn't see that.

"Naw, I don't see myself remarrying after losing Bill. He was the love of my life."

I wish to retract my insensitive question.

Two years ago, Josephine's husband had taken her parents to town. He had been drunk and ran head-on into a truck.

"You should come out and see my farm."

I pull into the parking lot at the printing service. "Yeah, that would be great," I say, not meaning it. "Hey, I am sorry the call is so short. I have to grab files for Marcus. Always on the run." A stupid laugh escapes me.

Josephine's voice drops. "Oh, that was a short call. Okay. Don't work too hard."

"You as well."

I balance my phone with the new screen protector between my ear and shoulder as I open the fridge and remove ingredients for ravioli.

"This is a crisis," Marcus's voice booms against my ear. He has almost hit level three tone. I grab a pot to fill with water.

"I need you in Hot Springs again this weekend."

Sure, Marcus, why not, Marcus? I don't want a life.

I look at the ingredients on the counter. I have lost the will to make dinner tonight. After being away from home for sixteen hours, I will order a burger to the house.

"This is the exit to Josephine's farm," I say to no one as I slow down. Josephine lives not too far off of US-70. I don't have to be in Hot Springs until tomorrow.

"What the heck, why not." I drive onto some hick-road. I hope Josephine likes impromptu visits. What does her farm look like? If I see neglected animals, will I turn her in? I might have to.

I pull into her driveway. Rocks click as my tires roll over them, and my vehicle comes to a stop. This driveway used to be a mud pit. Uncle Jack had to tow my parents out a couple of times. The gravel is an excellent addition since I was there for the funeral.

Four hounds announce my arrival as they lazily watch me get out of my vehicle. They lay on the porch, making noise but too complacent to move. My golden retriever, Lady, would jump on anyone on her territory.

I regret my high heels as I walk to the door. The spikey heel keeps sinking into the soft ground. If I had planned to visit Josephine, I would have brought more appropriate clothing. I go over my wardrobe in my head. I don't think I own one thing I could comfortably wear on a hillbilly farm. I could have picked something up at the thrift store before I came out. I shudder. I haven't worn used clothes since I moved out on my own.

I knock on the door, which appears to have a fresh coat of turquoise paint on it. *Wow, the door looks good.* The front exterior of the house has never been upkept or modern. Someone driving by might not realize a hillbilly lives here.

"Hello," I hear from the side of the house. Josephine comes towards me. At least, I think it's Josephine. The lady has a modern hairstyle with decent-looking clothing.

Before I finish smiling, Josephine charges at me. With a swoop, she lifts me and spins me around.

"Cathy! You came to see me."

My stomach churns to her spin, and yet she keeps going. A thousand years later, my feet touch the ground. I wobble on my high heels as my head steadies.

"I am so glad you came to visit me," Josephine speaks quickly. I had always thought of her like a slug with slow speech. Now, she sounds like a chipmunk with her squeaking and crazy fast pace.

She grabs my hand as if we were children and pulls me to the back of her property. Her callused skin scratches my hands. She isn't the soft cousin I saw two years ago.

Josephine gives me a tour of her farm, and I feel blown away. The animals appear healthy with shiny coats. They all have appropriate stalls or fenced enclosures. The farm seems like something a professional farmer with at least ten employees would run. How has one lone woman managed this farm, plus that woman being Josephine?

As we stand in front of dairy cows, I ask, "How many farm hands do you have working here?"

"Just me." Her eyes twinkle in pride.

"Just you? How can you run this huge farm by yourself?"

Josephine pats her chest. "Yup, lill' me."

Little was right. She looks as if she lost at least 80 pounds.

"Who helped you set up the farm? This looks way too amazing for you to have done on your own."

Josephine rocks back on her heels and puts her hands in her waistband. She pushes out her chin and smiles. "I set the whole thing up myself."

I cough as I choke on my spit. "The fences, the repairs to the barn? Everything?"

She licks her lips and smiles wider. "Just me."

I spin around. There is no way Josephine has done this—she is the laziest person I ever knew.

Does she wake up at 4 a.m. and go to bed at midnight? How can she run this place alone?

I can't hold back. "I don't mean to be a jerk, but Cuz, you are... You were the laziest person I ever knew. How can you keep up on a farm like this?"

Josephine stares at me to the point of discomfort.

I pull out my phone to check my emails and distract myself from her uncomfortable stare.

"Can you keep a secret?"

I look up from my phone. "Of course."

Josephine yanks my hand, and my phone flies into the cow pen.

She contemplates my bare legs and skirt. "I'll grab it for you," she says, crawling under the fence and rescuing my phone. She wipes the brown goop onto her pants and returns it to me.

Again, she grabs my free hand and drags me across her property.

My other hand burns as it holds my phone. *How can I ever use it again after it swam in a poopy field?*

Josephine stops. "Here is my secret."

This spot is a natural clearing from the trees.

What is secret about this? "I don't get it?"

Josephine points to the ground. "Look."

"Look at what? How is this a secret? Do you meditate in this clearing? How is this the secret to your farm?"

"That." Josephine points to a small, pooled area of water. Rocks surround it, almost like a vast firepit, yet filled with water.

"This is a natural spring," she says.

"Okay. So?"

"So, this spring invigorates me. It fills me with an energy unlike any you or I have ever felt before."

"Hmmm."

"You want to try it?"

It seems as if fatigue instantly hits me when she asks. I am not too far from Hot Springs, but I am ready to be done. Besides, *Eww!*

"Josephine, I am super proud of what you have done with this place. This doesn't at all look like the swamp I remember. Your animals are healthy. I am very proud of you." I look at my watch again. "I should be going. I have a big day tomorrow. I don't want to get to my hotel too late tonight."

"Just sleep here."

Instantly, a smell memory of ammonia and rotten food from her childhood home hits me. As a grown-up, I like things perfect. Why would I stay here when I have a luxurious room at Hot Springs waiting? Besides, the breakfast there can't compare to hillbilly-slop.

"I am fine. I don't want to impose."

Josephine grabs my shoulders and turns me to face her.

"I won't let you leave until you try this natural spring. It is warm and like a hot tub, but it is the secret to my success." Her eyes have changed. She looks possessed, and I step backward.

I flare my hands over my skirt. "I don't really have the right close for hot tubbing."

"You can borrow something of mine."

I almost reply that her clothes will drown me, then I realize we are about the same body size with her weight loss.

"I don't know…"

Josephine grabs my hand and drags me into her house to change clothes.

The warm water massages my legs. I'd finally agreed to Josephine's persistence. My usual self would balk at the grossness of sitting in a hillbilly cesspool, but I remind myself that spring water is known for having high mineral content that is excellent for the skin.

I sink completely up to my chin in water.

Water ripples as Josephine climbs in. She launches an inflatable pillow at me.

"Keep your arms up out of the water. Here, rest them on here," she says.

"Why?" I ask.

"Trust me."

I sit up and take my arms out. The cool night air chills them as little drops of water stick to my hairs. Vibrant flames dance from the Tiki poles propped around us. Their yellow hue reflects off Josephine's face. I forget and drop my arms back into the water.

Josephine grabs them and pulls them out.

"I ain't kidding, Cuz. Keep your arms out."

I question her with my eyes. "Why?"

"There is a reason, but I won't tell you just yet."

"That is odd."

"If you knew, then you might hop out of the water."

I hop out anyways. "That doesn't reassure me. Is there some sort of weird parasite in here?"

"No."

"Then tell me what you are hiding from me."

Josephine's face hardens. "Listen, there is magic in this water. You will find it gives you an energy unlike you have ever felt before. You will have the ability to accomplish everything you wish."

"That is stupid," I reply.

"Cathy, you know how lazy I am. I promise you; there is no way I could take care of this farm without the benefits of the water. They are real."

She has a point. I sit back in the water, placing my arms on the stupid inflatable pillow.

"Tell me the negative effects."

"I will. Just not yet. You need to truly feel the power of the water before I tell you the downfalls. They aren't big. But I don't want to scare you off."

I don't trust her, but her farm speaks loudly as evidence of what she proclaims.

I forget my trepidations within seconds as the pleasurable warmth penetrates all my submerged muscles. I rarely give myself breaks from life where I simply relax. Even if nothing more comes out of this, I am glad to relax

In Josephine's spare room, I can't sleep. My mind races like a supercomputer fresh out of the box. I pull out my laptop and solve ten dilemmas from work with ease. I complete all I can on the laptop then do pushups, sit-ups, and a few other exercises. I feel great. I haven't worked out in years. Usually, when I get home from work, I am too exhausted to do much more than order food in and either work on my laptop or go to bed.

The next day in Hot Springs with my clients, it surprises me to feel this energetic. I haven't felt so full of life, well, ever. And here I am, without sleep, and feeling like someone shot me with solar flares from the sun.

On the way home, I can hardly sit still for the drive. I want to hop out of the car and run home. The other annoying part of the drive is the intense itch I have all over my body. I scratch and scratch, probably a little too vigorously, since I have nothing else to do. I must be allergic to the farm.

It's Tuesday and flowers arrive from Marcus. They are a mix of lilies and sunflowers. What a perfect combination. Who did he have to order them? That was usually my job. He sent them because I had gone into the office Sunday evening, too antsy to stay home. I rearranged his office and mine. I sorted through files he had been pestering me about. By the time I left the office tonight, it seems as if I had accomplished everything on the backlogged to-do list.

And then it hit.

I crash.

All that good energy disappears, and I feel like something has come and sucked my soul out of my body.

It's Wednesday, and I can't get out of bed.

"I don't care that you are sick. Wait, I shouldn't say that. I care. But that is beside the point. If I care or don't doesn't impact that I need that Smith case finished by three. At least you can log on and finish it from home." Marcus' voice is almost a level three.

"I have never called into work before. You can be more kind."

I hang up on him and let my phone slip onto the bed next to me. He wants me to do a report. I just want to die. The phone rings and rings, but I can't answer it. I drift to sleep.

It's Thursday, and I can't believe I have to call into work again.

What is going on? Am I sick? Have I contracted a parasite from Josephine's hot tub?

I can't function.

Josephine's hot tub would restore me back to life.

I need to get back to it, but I don't have the energy to drive.

I discover La Fun Bus, which shuttles to Hot Springs Friday morning.

The bus driver agrees to drop me off at Josephine's exit and she picks me up. She almost has to carry me to the spring water because traveling has zapped the last of my energy.

Instantaneously, after sitting in the warm spring water, life returns to me.

"What is going on?" I ask.

Josephine smiles sheepishly. "I told you there were side effects."

My hand goes into the water, and I scratch my waistline.

Josephine watches me scratch myself. "How ya dealing with that one?"

"Which one?"

"The itching?"

"Oh, it is driving me insane. It has been a week since I was in this water. Why does it still itch?"

"I hate to tell you; the skin will be a constant problem. There will be a day when you wish it was just a lill' itch."

I finish scratching my belly. "What do you mean?"

Josephine looks at me and then toward her farm. "I don't think I'll tell you. You will learn soon enough."

"That is dumb, just tell me."

Josephine faces me.

"Naw."

We relax, which is an interesting term because my energy levels rise. I had felt like I had clawed my way out of a grave just a few moments before. Now, I have the super energy of wonder woman.

"Do you always get that tired after the effects of the water wear off?"

"It gets worse," she says.

"Worse, I don't think I can deal with worse."

"It isn't bad for me because I never let that happen. As soon as I start to feel the energy dissipate, I come and resoak."

"So, would you say the exhaustion gets worse?"

"Way worse."

I slump into the water. Josephine grabs my arms and places them on the inflatable pillow. "Trust me, you don't want those getting into the water."

I think about the itch, and realize she is right. I don't want that intense itch on my arms.

I enter the kitchen, and a huge spread of breakfast is laid out before me. It smells better in here than a café.

"All from the farm," Josephine smiles as she flips an egg. "Come, eat."

Bacon, ham, hashbrowns, eggs, and pancakes.

"That is a lot of food for the two of us."

Josephine picks at a pancake corner and eats it as she finishes cooking the eggs.

"Between the both of us, we can down this."

"How have you lost so much weight?"

I sit, and Josephine brings me a plate of food fit to feed a lumberjack.

"The power of the water. I eat whatever I want, and the weight never returns."

I pinch my soft middle. I wouldn't mind that.

Josephine's hillbilly side shines through as she shovels the food in. Runny egg yolk dribbles down her chin. *So gross.*

"What made you decide to farm?" I delicately take a bite of my eggs. Rich flavor burst from their liquidy delight. She had cooked them perfectly.

"Not long after I discovered the spring, I decided to farm."

"You mean, you came up with the farm after you discovered the spring water?"

"Sure did. I was go'n crazy."

"Wait, you have lived here all your life. Didn't you guys know anything about the spring before?"

"The spring was an underground spring. When I was digging holes for Ma' and Pa's bodies, I uncovered the spring."

Creepy. Goosebumps erupt on me.

I bathe in oatmeal and chamomile, trying to stop the intense burning. The itching had turned to burning. This must be what Josephine meant when she said I would wish it was just an itch. My red skin screams angrily from everywhere I have ripped up with my nails.

I hate the pin-point black dots all over my body. At first, I thought they were ticks. They looked as small as seed ticks, but thankfully they weren't. Now, they almost look like a rash, except, well, they are black. Maybe that is why my skin burns.

When I wake up, all I want to do is call 911 to take me to the morgue. I can't handle the exhaustion, nor can I wait until Friday for it to get worse. I board the bus and go to Josephine's house.

"You might have to move in," she tells me. She appears fresh and full of life.

I sit in the water, and almost instantly, life returns.

"I can't move to this small town of nothing," I say. "What would I do?"

"You could help me run the farm. I don't actually need help, but we could expand it and get more animals. Imagine that. You and me! We used to dream about moving together when we were kids."

My heart races, and my fingers tingle at the thought. I would go insane living in such a small town. I love Memphis, Tennessee. I crave the hustle and bustle. Besides, I ain't no hillbilly.

Restored with the power of the spring, I return to work, and I rock my job. I slip into public relations and pick up assignments with media relations as well. Essentially, I work three titles at once. Marcus buys me jewelry, dinners, and lots of bonuses.

Two months passed.

I now have to go to Josephine's twice a week.

I have no choice.

"I really need you there, Cathy. How can you let me down?"

I stand in front of Marcus with twenty files tucked under my right armpit while my left arm holds two Tennessee Code & Statues books. I ignore the ringing phone, which balances on the books, threatening to fall and cost me another screen repair.

"You should answer that. What if it is a client?" Marcus demands.

"I have voicemail. Besides, I am in a meeting with my boss."

"Oh yes, anyways, I need you on the boating outing with the Pecos. You will secure them as a client, not me. You have the looks—the words. You have people skills. I can't do this without you. Besides, I will be busy driving the boat, so I won't be up to making deals."

I had always gone on his boating expeditions. He pulled out the boat whenever he tried to reel in a new client or retain one threatening to leave.

"I can't," I say as I turn my back to him. I struggle telling Marcus no. He has power over me. Not attraction. But he controls me with his position as my boss.

"Don't blow this for me."

"Marcus, I do the work of three employees now. You will be fine without me."

"No, Cathy, I won't. As your boss, I order you to go." Marcus takes the files from me. With my hand now free, I scratch my abdomen. The burning feels like my skin is sizzling away.

I look away in shame. I really want to go. I love his boat parties, but there is no way that I can.

I turn my back to him and walk away. "Bring Patty. I promise I will not be there."

Marcus screams at a level three. "If you don't come, you are fired!"

Marcus, such a toddler!

"I would like to see you fire me," I say as I walk out of his office.

Like most drives to Josephine's, I struggle. The lethargy threatens to close my eyes and shut down all my body functions.

"I almost didn't make it," I say after the water revitalizes me. "I might have to start coming three times a week."

"Yes, I believe you will."

My stomach drops. I make this drive at night now. The roundtrip, including the soak, takes about seven to eight hours. I do it in an entire night.

"I am not lying when I say you should move here."

"I can't leave my life."

Josephine rubs the top of her head then looks back at me.

"Cathy, I hate to tell you this, but it will come to a point where you will need to soak in the water every day. You will be making this trip every single night."

Gloom!

What!

How can that be true?

Every night.

"I can't drive back and forth for eight hours every night!"

We sit in silence, and I think about Marcus' disappointment in me. He will be taking the Pecos on the boat tomorrow at noon, and I really do want to go. I will be back in time, but there is just no way.

"What do you do about the black spots on your skin?" I ask. "My boss needed me to go boating with him tomorrow, but there is just no way."

"What point are they at?"

I stand and lift my shirt. Black spots the size of a screw heads cover the entirety of my body, except my chest up, and arms. The places Josephine had instructed me to keep out of the water.

"Lucky, I wish my blackness was still at that stage."

Her words send out an alarm. "Can I see your black spots?"

Josephine lifts her tank top. "I wouldn't call them spots anymore." The entirety of her skin looks like worn, black leather. I cautiously rub it. So dry and rough.

My hand recoils.

"Yup, your skin will eventually look like this."

Dark, hot anger builds from my toes and wants to rip out of my face. I can hardly control the rage as I drive. Lately, it has been harder to manage my tempter. But now, I have a legitimate reason for this.

"I don't want to drive here three nights a week," I scream into the steering wheel. I sound more like Marcus than me.

Josephine's words repeat in my head. "Cathy, I hate to tell you this, but it will come to a point where you will need to soak in the water every day. You will be making this trip every single night."

"I can't do this. I can't drive here every night." I pass stretches of nothing. "I can't move here. That is not an option."

"Ahhhh!" My throat aches from the velocity of my scream. My fists pound the steering wheel.

"I don't want this anymore. Sure, I love the high from the water, but the downs are hell. I am trapped. Trapped to this."

I flip the dome light on and look at my ashen face in the visor mirror. The dim light washes out my already gaunt face. Big black bags billow around my eyes, flat eyes that no longer spark life. They appear sad, almost zombie-like. My cheeks have sunk in from losing over twenty pounds.

I do, however, love the insurmountable energy, being able to accomplish a million projects. That is amazing. I love the accolades of my coworkers who can't come close to keeping up with me. I lavish the gifts and recognition from Marcus.

But is it worth it?

I had never seen anything as disgusting as Josephine's skin. Mine is pretty grotesque, but her revolting skin is my future.

Marcus pouts like a four-year-old. "You can't use your time off."

"My legal contract states I get four weeks off a year. Now, Mr. Wollen, I know you believe in upholding the law to the fullest," I say.

"But I need you. Can't you just work a little? I mean, you are going to be home. Please, at least do a little each day."

"Nope, working will get in the way of my staycation."

I finish things at my office, and by the time I stop, I think I will collapse on the floor. I call an Uber to take me home.

I open the door to my apartment, and Lady jumps on me and knocks me to the ground. I kick the door closed.

I can't move out of pure depletion. Every cell in my body not only aches, but they feel as if they have deflated. I had reached this point before, this being the most horrific feeling ever.

It has been over two years since I naively dipped into the spring water.

I have to soak in the water every day now. This destroys my life. I made firm rules to Marcus that I have to leave work no later than 9 p.m. There are always constant dinner meetings and social events he demands I go to. I have no choice. I have to miss them. If I don't drive to Josephine's, I will be worthless by 2 a.m.

I had gotten into a wreck once when I allowed Marcus to talk me into going to a dinner. I didn't leave until after midnight. At two in the morning, the exhaustion hit me, and I couldn't operate the vehicle. My car went off the road and slammed into a tree. I voice activated a call to Josephine, and she came and got me. I didn't want to get the insurance or police involved.

"Cathy," the police had said to me on the phone the next day. "We found your car crashed into..."

"You found my car!" I said in delight. "It was stolen last night. Oh good, where did you find it?"

"In Arkansas, just off of..."

I'd interrupted again. "I live in Tennessee. What was my car doing in Arkansas?"

As I lay in my entryway, too exhausted to move, the dogs and cats walk all over me. I fall in and out of sleep for the next two days. My racing heart and the profuse sweating keep waking me up. Everything aches on me. I even hallucinate.

Dark, ugly depression settles in me, like a monster who refuses to leave. Honestly, I would kill myself without hesitation if I could, but I can't move from my spot in the entryway.

Six days later, my door opens. I force my dry eyes open and make out feet.

Everything goes dark.

The energy is better than I had ever known. I open my eyes as I marinate in Josephine's springs.

"How did I get here?"

"I came and got you," Josephine said.

"How did you know I needed you?"

"When you missed the first night, I worried. Then, with each executive night you missed, I knew you were in trouble."

"Thanks," I say. Do I mean it? It felt good to have the life restored to me, but on the other hand, she had stopped me from detoxing. By Josephine bringing me here, I had been unsuccessful and will have to go through all that over again.

"I want to be done," I say.

"I know you do."

"I can't do this anymore."

"I get it."

Josephine looks understanding but not empathetic.

I ask, "Have you ever tried to quit?"

"Three times."

"Obviously, without success," I say, waving to her.

"I once went forty days free from the water."

"Wow, I guess that is commendable."

"No. It isn't. I lay in my bed in the most excruciating pain, unable to do anything. I wished for death, but it didn't come. It was like the worst hell I could imagine. I was aware of all my pain but without the ability to do anything about it. At one point, I blacked out, and when I came to, I was in the water. I don't know how I got there. I must have found some reserve and crawled there." She shrugged her shoulders. "Who knows. But when my energy restored..." Her voice chokes up. "I found all my animals dead." Tears stream down her face. "No one had cared for them while I was detoxing."

She wipes her eyes and looks back at me. "Detoxing. I don't think that is possible. I don't think I will ever escape the adverse side effects of being out of the water. I am tethered to this water pit for life. Like a marriage. For better or for worse."

Never being able to detoxify, sounds unspeakable. Tied to this water for the rest of my life. What a hell.

"Cathy, I have something to tell you."

She should have a lot to tell me. Why has she withheld any of this from me?

"Your dogs and cats died while you were detoxing. Only one dog was alive. I gave him water, but he isn't doing well. I brought him back with us."

My heart sinks. "No. Not my pets. Not my family. Please tell me the dog that lived was Lady." I can't handle this.

"If Lady is a boy."

I pound the water with my hands and slip chin deep into the water.

"Cathy, you don't want to get your visible skin wet. You don't want the water to change your skin."

I turn to her with venom in my words. "What does it matter?"

"Oh, it matters," she says, removing my arms.

I hit her arms away. "Why did you do this to me?"

"Why did I save you?"

"No. Why did you let me dip in your hell? WHY? You knew the consequences, and yet you had me partake. WHY?"

Josephine won't look at me. "I dunno. I thought you would like the power of it all."

"You thought I wanted to be chained to this hell?"

"Yeah, I guess. I love my farm, and I wouldn't be able to do it without this stream."

"Josephine, even you tried to detox but couldn't. You knew about it all. About the damage to the skin. About the never-ending hell of withdrawal. About the tiredness and exhaustion. Why did you damn me?"

"I dunno. I guess I hoped that one day you would move in with me and help me run the farm." Josephine's voice chokes up. "I am so lonely out here all alone."

"Then move," I say.

Josephine drops her eyes. "I can't. I have to live by the water. I am trapped in its clutches. I am at the point where I have to dip every twelve hours now."

"So, that is my future in two years?"

"I am afraid so."

"Why did you do this to me?"

"I told you, I hated being alone."

"You purposely dragged me into your hell."

"I am sorry."

"No, you are not!"

I run out of her pond and to the driveway.

Crap, my car isn't here.

I open the door to her truck, and as I suspect, the keys dangle from the ignition.

The truck roars to life and I peel out of the driveway. I see Josephine madly waving after me.

"Screw you, Cuz!" I scream with an intensity that shreds my throat.

I drive onto the dark night road. I don't go far when I pull over.

Where will I go?

What will I do?

I just want to go home, but what is the point? To drive back tonight. Besides, my babies are dead.

"Just look at the nothingness here." If I move to Josephine's, my professional life is over.

"No more suits. No more heels. No more power-lunches."

All the prestige I have built will end.

My life will end.

But what kind of life is this?

It's a hell.

I can't keep driving to Josephine's. And before I know it, nightly won't be enough.

I am not a farmer.

Josephine couldn't detox after forty days. This addiction is in my life forever.

I slam my hand into her steering wheel.

My life is hell, and now I am eternally shackled to a hillbilly farm in Arkansas.

What will I do?

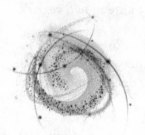

ABOUT THE AUTHOR

When Stephanie Daich isn't hiking a mountain or sparring in MMA, she brings the thrill of life to her writing.

SOMETHING ELSE TO DO
BY
STEVEN D. BREWER

SOMETHING ELSE TO DO

I really shouldn't have stayed up all night. By the time I got through my shift at the restaurant, I could barely focus on anything and was starting to see double. Or were those auras around everything? Getting away from the lights eased my overloaded senses and helped me focus.

I went past the park benches into the wooded border with the cemetery. Someone had gone through my stuff again. This time, however, they had torn open the plastic bags and dumped out everything I had. Seemingly, they hadn't taken anything — it was just dirty clothes and a few paperback books after all. I didn't think it was going to rain overnight, so I just laid down under the tarp and went to sleep. At least, I planned to.

It should have been easy. I was so tired I couldn't keep my eyes open. Or I couldn't shut my eyes. After a bit, I stood up and started dancing along with the music. While I danced, I gathered up my clothes and sorted them into piles. Colors. Whites. Socks.

"You should put the socks in with the whites," she said.

"I thought they'd bleed," I said.

"Maybe if they were new," she said. "But washing the socks in hot is a good idea."

"Who said anything about washing?" I said, dancing in circles as I took each book, opened it, and set it like a roof on each pile of clothes.

"Why are you dancing anyway?" she said.

"Ssh!" I said. "I like this song."

My dancing had taken me out of the woods and into the park, where there was more space to move around. This was my favorite part of the song, and I lifted my arms over my head and kicked up my heels, turning round and around in time with the music.

"I still don't hear any song," she said.

"Ssh! Ssh!" I said. "Don't talk for a minute."

An elderly couple was approaching on the sidewalk, and I closed my eyes to focus on the music and my dance.

"Don't shush me!" she said. "I can talk if I want to!"

The elderly couple stepped to the side, eyeing me nervously, edged past, and then hurried away.

"Why did you have to do that?" I said. "That was the best part of the song."

"What do I care?" she said. "I'm dead anyway."

"But I'm not."

"That's your problem," she said bitterly.

I followed the sidewalk to an old playground. The equipment was run down and broken. It was dinnertime and the kids, if any still used this place, had gone home. I sat down on a rusty swing.

"What do you mean 'you're dead' anyway?" I asked.

"I'm dead. I'm not among the living. I'm a ghost."

"Baa! Baa!" I said making horns with my fingers.

"I said 'ghost,' you asshole."

"If you're dead, why are you still here?"

"I think it's because I have a lingering regret," she said. "I never got to see the sun set over the ocean."

"That's hard to do in New York."

"That's why I need to get to California."

"Wouldn't Florida be closer?"

"The Gulf of Mexico is not the ocean," she said flatly.

"Well, you can't argue with logic like that. But how are you going to get there?"

"Let's go together."

"You're serious. You want me to just drop everything and take you to California. So you can see the sun set over the ocean."

"Are you doing something else?"

"You've got a point," I admitted. "I guess we should hit the road."

For the first time in months, I went home. It was weird walking through the pretty residential neighborhood where I had grown up. The yards and streets were deserted, and all the windows were dark. It was 3 a.m., after all.

"Wow. Nice neighborhood," she said.

"Ssh. You really need to be quiet for a few minutes, because if you wake anyone up, this is going to be the shortest trip in history." I knew if my parents discovered me, they'd call the police and I'd end up back *there*. And I didn't want to go *there* again.

The spare key was still under the brick, where it always was. I quietly unlocked the door into the garage, replaced the key, then quietly slipped in and locked the door behind me. The house was silent.

I pulled the cover off my motorcycle. And it was my motorcycle. I had bought it myself, before... I put on the helmet that was sitting on the seat. I ran my fingers over the bike lovingly. It was a large bike, made for cruising and long-distance highway trips. I checked that the gas was turned on and primed.

I knew it would wake up the house, but I pushed the garage door button anyway. As soon as the door was high enough for the bike, I pushed it under the door and ducked my head. Once I was clear, I mounted the bike and, as it rolled down the driveway, I kicked the starter. It took three tries, because the bike hadn't been run for a while, but then it fired up and began to purr. What a beautiful sound! I let the bike idle in the street until the garage door was fully open, then pushed the button again and it started going down as lights came on in the house. Then, I put in the clutch, kicked it into first, and we cruised out of the neighborhood.

Dawn found us on the expressway headed west. The sun came up behind us casting long shadows. I was careful to stay with the flow of traffic and not speed — until we hit the less populated areas farther west.

We crossed the eastern United States. We cut through southern Pennsylvania and the low mountains of West Virginia. We hit Columbus by early evening and Indianapolis at midnight. Swarms of tiny bugs rose up from the fields in the early hours of the morning as we crossed the huge agricultural fields of Indiana and Illinois. By sunrise, we had crossed the Mississippi and were in Missouri.

We pulled off whenever the gas started to get low. I had just gotten paid, so I had enough money to fill the gas tank and grab some cheap burgers and then take a piss before pressing on.

I really opened the throttle when we got to Oklahoma. We sped through the Panhandle State and northern Texas as the land got more arid and rocky. We crossed New Mexico and Arizona in the afternoon. We reached western California, running out of gas — and out of money.

As dusk fell, I saw the neon lights for a roadside bar switch on up ahead. The Tumbleweed. Live Blues Music. I downshifted and turned in.

It was the first place I'd seen in a couple of hours. The building looked pretty sketchy, but the parking lot was full — always a good sign. I found a spot to park the motorcycle, took off the helmet and, after a few moments stretching, went inside.

There was no place to sit, so I found a place to hover near the bar. Next to me, a small knot of people were trying to talk over the noise.

"What are we going to do?" said one, a tall, thin blond man.

"I can't sing for shit," said another, a short trans woman wearing goth makeup and black nail polish.

"We can't play without a vocalist," said another, a burly man with a thick, closely cropped beard.

"Excuse me," she said. "Do you need a vocalist?"

"Ssh! Ssh!" I said.

All four heads turned toward me. The last was a bald man who was unbelievably ripped, with bulging muscles everywhere. With their eyes on me, I felt like sinking into the floor, and looked down, unable to meet their eyes.

"Can you sing?" said the burly man, who was evidently the bandleader.

"I… Uh…" I said.

"Oh, yeah," she cut in. "I can sing the blues. Nobody better."

"We do a lot of old Jennifer Boone covers. Can you do that?"

"You bet. I know them all! Just give me a try," she said.

"OK. What's your name?"

"Anderson Jones," I said finally, after she didn't reply.

They took the stage and started tuning up. The blond man played lead guitar and the trans woman was on rhythm. The burly man played bass. The guy with the muscles played the drums. They got tuned up and then the drummer stood and said, "Welcome to the Tumbleweed. We're the Blues Mechanics. I'm

Bruce on Bass. Introducing Robbie on lead, Jerzy on rhythm, and Sticks on the drums. And tonight only, we have Anderson Jones sitting in for Sandy. And now let's get started!"

The lead guitar played the opening notes. I had been standing there with the microphone in my hand, staring at the floor and not sure what to do. But once the music started, I couldn't stop myself and I began to dance. Then the rhythm guitar came in. And then the bass. And when the drums started, I did a set of cartwheels across the stage. And then she started to sing.

"Without you, baby, the sun will never rise…"

I had never heard this song before, but I loved it. The beat was hypnotic, and I felt it reach down into someplace deep in my heart.

"Without you, baby, all hope inside me dies…"

Her voice control was amazing. She held me and the audience spellbound with her vocal performance. The band was good and tight, but it was her voice that people responded to emotionally.

When she got to the chorus, "Come back, baby! I need you by my side!" the whole audience came to their feet and joined in. The musicians were all looking at each other with astonishment.

We played one set, took a short break, and then played another. As the final chord sounded, I was frozen looking down. There was a momentary silence and then the audience came to their feet and erupted into cheers.

The band surrounded me, clapping me on the back. Jerzy hugged me and I hugged her back. I sobbed and tears ran down my face and onto her shoulder.

"Hey! Hey! That was incredible! I've never felt it so much before!" she said.

"The audience loved you! You're a hit! You're a bigger hit than Sandy was!" Bobby pounding me on the back.

I still couldn't find any words and just nodded, looking down.

"I told you I could sing the blues," she said. "It comes with the territory."

The manager of the bar came over with an envelope and handed it to Bruce.

"Here's your fee," he said. "I gotta say, that was the best show you've ever done. I'm sorry I can't pay you any more, but if you want to grab a bite to eat, it's on me. Just put in your order before the kitchen closes."

They dragged me to the bar, and we gave our orders to the pretty waitress chewing gum. She read back the order, punctuating each statement by pointing the eraser on her pencil toward each of us in turn. Then we took a table to the side. The place had mostly emptied out with the show over, although there were still no seats at the bar.

"You couldn't know this," Robbie said, "but Sandy messaged us just before the show to say she was ditching us."

"That bitch!" Jerzy said. "She could have told us sooner, and we wouldn't have dragged our asses all the way out here."

"But then we'd never have met you," Bruce said to me. "I think what I'm saying — and I think I speak for everyone..."

He paused and looked at Sticks, who just nodded.

"Would you be interested in becoming our new vocalist?" he continued.

"I... Uh... I don't know," I said.

"I've got something I need to do," she said. "And I'm not sure it would work out after that."

Everyone looked downcast. A pall started to settle over the table.

"Well... Uh... Can I think about it?" I asked.

"You can always leave a message for me there," Bruce said, handing me a card. Then he got out the envelope and pulled out a thick sheaf of cash.

"Sandy always demanded half of the fee," he continued, handing me 20 large bills. "And since you saved us, we should give you what she would have taken."

"Oh, no," I said. "No, I couldn't. Let's split it evenly."

I took eight and put the others on the table. They divvied up the rest of the money and then our food came, and we ate. I wolfed mine down and then stood to leave.

"I gotta run," I said.

"Thanks for letting me sit in," she said. "I haven't had that much fun in a long time."

They waved, somewhat wistfully, as I hit the door.

It was nearly midnight when I fired up the motor and, after filling the gas tank, we got back on the road. By sunrise we were in San Bernardino and fighting rush hour traffic in LA. It took hours, creeping along through 6 lanes of stop-and-go traffic, to reach Long Beach.

"We've still got hours before sunset," I said. "Wanna go out to Catalina Island? The ferry is right there."

"Sure," she said. "As long as we can watch the sunset over the ocean."

The ferry was fast and comfortable. After we arrived in Avalon, we spent the afternoon hanging out on the boardwalk and walking along the beach. Neither of us had much to say as we watched the normies playing in the surf and sunbathing.

As the sun started to approach the horizon, I found a good vantage point to sit on an isolated breakwater and dangle my feet where waves would splash them every so often.

"I've read that if you watch at just the right moment when the sun sets over the ocean, you'll see a green flash," I said. "In that pirate movie, it's when a soul comes back from the dead."

"How ironic," she said.

"I know, right?"

We watched the sun get lower and lower. The wind died down as if the whole world was holding its breath.

"Don't blink," she said.

The sun slipped below the horizon and evening sprang into the sky with brilliant yellows and oranges and reds. But no green flash. I sat there for a long time until the bats came out and began to fly up and down the beach. And then the land breeze set up.

"Goodbye," I said. "I hope you find peace."

After several days awake, I finally felt like I could sleep and laid down on the beach. I closed my eyes and slept a dreamless sleep until the sun cleared the island the following morning.

"G'morning, sleepyhead," she said, as I stirred.

"Good morning," I said, yawning. "Wait a minute! Hold on! I thought you were gone. I thought your lingering regret was not seeing the sun set over the ocean!"

"It was," she said. "But now my lingering regret is not seeing the green flash."

"And you expect me to just hang around here until you see the green flash?"

"Are you doing something else?"

"You've got a point," I admitted. "I guess we should give the Blues Mechanics a call."

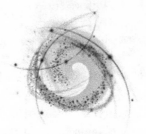

ABOUT THE AUTHOR

Steven D. Brewer teaches scientific writing at the University of Massachusetts Amherst. As an author, Brewer identifies diverse obsessions that underlie his writing: deep interests in natural history, life science, and environmentalism; an abiding passion for languages; a fascination with Japanese culture; and a mania for information technology and the Internet. Brewer lives in Amherst, Massachusetts with his extended family.

THE SIGHT
BY
DARBY COX

THE SIGHT

I arrive home with two bags in my hands.

One is a faded red duffle with black straps straining at the seams with all the clothing and shoes I own.

The other, smaller bag carries something I can never seem to leave behind. Something that rouses me every time I stumble upon it. Though, stumble doesn't feel like the right word. I worry I go looking for it. When I lay my fingers on its rough and worn cover, I remember *them*—feelings and memories long buried under the daily fears and worries of my life.

The bag swishes in the breeze, sweeping against my leg, crinkling as plastic does. A sharp jab to my thigh reminds me I need to get a new one—one without holes. The thought of losing the leatherbound book it holds sends a distressing flurry through me and I dash to the small shop inside the bus station.

"Could I get a plastic bag?" I ask the young woman behind the counter. When she turns around, she gasps.

"Adam? Adam Whistler?" Her eyes narrow as if that helps her make the connection between my clean-shaven defined jaw and freshly buzzed head and my younger face with its floppy brown hair and rounder cheeks scraped from racing through the woods.

I offer a blank expression in hopes she takes that as a no.

She doesn't.

"It's me, Jackie Simms. You used to babysit me when you were in high school. Do you remember?" She looks hopeful. My shoulders sag in response.

"Yeah. Hey Jackie, how are you?"

She squeals and my body cringes from my toes to the fuzz on my head.

"Wow I can't believe it's you. I'm doing fine. Working here and going to school at the community college in Waterford. Last I heard you moved to the city for college and were working some big corporate job with an energy company or something?"

A big corporate job with an energy company...or something. I did four years of expensive university, spent countless hours studying and preparing and banging my head against the wall to get an internship after graduation. All for everything to end up the way it did.

"Yeah, yeah, for a little bit."

"Cool. What brings you back to Trickle?"

I groan inwardly. All I want is the plastic bag she's holding hostage. But it's clear the cost is answers to her probing questions. Answers that will be texted to everyone she knows the minute I turn my back. Soon the whole town will know Adam Whistler finally showed up after his dad has been sick and alone for years. That's how it goes in small towns. Especially Trickle, the real name of which is Cumberland, named after the large river nearby. Ironic considering there are about 3,000 people here at a time, it is nowhere near any major roads, and only survives by siphoning resources off the nearby larger towns in the county. Hence, Trickle.

"Seeing my dad," I admit, though she already knows.

"Aw, glad to hear. We've all been wondering when you'd come back."

I'll never understand how small-town people don't see saying something like that as rude and invasive. I'm already yearning for the cold, stand-offish air of the city.

"Could I..." I motion towards the bag.

She gives me a laugh that is way too much for the moment and hands it over. I offer a nod as thanks, as I'm sure any word I utter will only inspire more conversation, then turn away.

"Good to see you! Try not to go running off into the woods looking for fairies!" she calls after me. My legs attempt to freeze up, but I force them to keep going.

More than having to provide a recap of the last eleven years to every person I come across, more than dodging the judging looks about the cruel son who didn't come home when his dad became gravely ill, I dread the whispers and raised eyebrows. The sneers and chuckles. The memories of gripping a leatherbound notebook with sweaty fingers as I scurried through town with my head down, hoping to avoid the older kids. When they inevitably saw me, their bike wheels would screech to a halt. I'd keep going, hoping slumped shoulders and a bowed head would deter them.

It never did.

Within minutes, I'd be flat on my back. Bramble and chunks of broken glass pricking into my skin through my shirt, but I didn't move. I'd wait on the ground while they tore the thick pages from the spine of the notebook, tossing them into the air while they howled their disapproval.

This isn't what boys like.

This isn't normal.

I'd lie there, listening for the sound of their bikes to wane down the road before climbing to my feet on trembling legs.

Pages littering the tall grass around me, swirling softly between the blades like curious butterflies.

Detailed drawings of a girl flying into the sky, quick sketches of rooftops below, puffy clouds above.

A soft, wonderous smile on her face as she looks to the tangerine and lavender heavens calling to her.

"You didn' need to come," Dad growls at me from behind the screen door. Even through the silvery black waves I can see the sallow, drooping skin of his cheeks, the red-pocked whites of his eyes, the way his jawline quivers under the weight of his scowl. He doesn't unlock the door, even as my hand reaches for the knob.

Yes, I know this isn't my home. I can't just walk in like I live here. I get it.

His point made, the lock clicks and he harumphs and hobbles out of the way.

I step into a sun-bathed living area, goldenrod beams of light granting much-needed charm to the otherwise cluttered room. It reeks of tobacco and stale beer. The T.V. is on a local news channel—by local I mean Waterford which is the next town thirty-seven miles away.

Dad lowers himself slowly into the chair directly in front of the T.V. A small tray next to it holds everything he covets in life. The remote, a lighter, his roll-up kit, a bag of dry tobacco, and the same glass ash tray he's had since I used to sleep behind the door at the end of the hall.

"Interestin' isn' it," he coughs out.

I clench, waiting for it to begin. "What is?"

"That you're the one who came back. Your sister and mother haven' even called."

I instinctively dodge his gaze.

"Are ya just going to stand there in my doorway and stare at the floor?"

Not even a minute has passed, and I already feel like a cat after someone runs their hands the opposite way of its fur. If I had the money I would be staying at the inn on the edge of town, but I don't. So, I'm here.

"Where am I staying?" I respond, matching his cadence. Challenging it even. I'm over six feet tall now, my shoulders are broad, my head is shaved. I'm not the scrawny teenager who fled a decade ago.

And he can tell. He eyes me out of his periphery, sizing me up. Trying to figure out how many pointed comments he can get away with.

"Nothin's changed."

That means I'm to go to the room at the end of the hall. I cross the living area, briefly blocking the T.V.—he grunts and attempts to crane his neck around as if that one second lost is a great affront—and the plastic bag catches on the chunk of chipped wood sticking out of his arm rest.

The book tumbles out, littering all the loose pages stuffed between the thick covers.

He sees it all.

Then he says something which is lost over the pounding of my heart in my ears.

My first instinct is to scramble to collect them, to protect the drawings from his appalled eyes. Yet I'm overcome with the urge to puff my torso out, jut my shoulders back.

You're not a little boy anymore. He can't make you feel like shit.

"My god. You still doin' this shit?" he laughs, but it's not the least bit funny. Despite all my years away, my height, my width, my shaved head, I wince.

I'm on my knees the next second, scooping up every trace of my shame. He kicks at one that found itself under his chair, as if it's a cockroach. I swipe it before his grime-covered shoes leave stains on her.

Without another word I storm down the hall, thunderous and threatening, slamming the door closed for extra measure. It doesn't work. Through the wood I can hear him muttering about faeries, the woods behind our house, something, something, not what men do.

My cheeks feel hot, and I dig my fingers into the inflamed skin. Maybe nothing has changed. Because I'm angry and embarrassed. I'm once again twelve years old, face-up in the dirt as the town laughs at me, mocks me.

More importantly I've told him, the taunting boys, the giggling girls, the rude old ladies and snarling old men, time and time again that she's not a fairy.

She's something else entirely.

I shouldn't do this. This isn't why I came back.

But what if?

My sweat-slicked palm nearly slides off the doorknob as it turns. Creaks from the old door swinging open echo off the yellowed walls of the hallway. I wince, hoping it doesn't seep through Dad's bedroom door.

Silence settles over the house for a few moments before I decide its safe.

One unsure foot in front of the other, I steal across the small, one-story home to the front door. It isn't until I reach the screen that I remember I'm an adult. I don't need to sneak out at night for fear my father will catch me scampering off into the woods again.

The first time I was caught, I naively thought he was worried about wolves and black bears, but that hope was ripped from my fingers along with my book. I stood in the middle of the living room as he flipped through every drawing, ranting about weirdness, and girly shit, and never finding a job.

With one last glance back at my father's still door, I slip through the cracked entrance…making sure it closes with the faintest of squeaks.

My feet know exactly where to go. They take me down the front steps to the well-walked path around the back of the house. When I was a kid, this path was open, cleared of overhanging trees and debris because my sister and I often played here. Now, I'm hopping over rusted car parts, old lawn chairs, and batting away low hanging branches before they can catch on my clothes.

The path takes me to a backyard with a low deck and the skeleton of what once was a trampoline. A little flutter appears in my chest at the memory of jumping as high as my scrawny legs could take me. I wanted to be closer to the sky. Closer to her.

It takes me a bit to find a way through, the grass so tall and unruly it snags on the lower buttons of my jacket. When I finally find it, a thin, overgrown foot path leading into the nearby woods, a thick ball of phlegm forms in my throat.

I can still turn back now. Forget this childish whim ever took hold of me.

Before my brain decides, I'm already crossing a small field towards the wall of barbed black spikes ahead. Peeks of dove white moonlight between thin trunks guide me across the acorn and moss-blanketed floor. The terrain rolls up and down in soft waves, trees rising and falling like cresting ships. Brisk air bites at my fingertips, so I tuck them into my pockets and keep my gaze glued to the footpath.

In summers past, I took this very journey every night I could, with one hand gripping an old yellow flashlight and the other clutching my book to my chest.

I couldn't get myself to bring it. That was too much. That felt like admitting.

The forest floor begins to slope upwards, and my knees and ankles bend to dig into the crumbling rock and pinecones. By the time I start to see flickering lights from the town below, I'm panting. I spot my house a ways down from the main strip of businesses that make up all jobs in Trickle. Grocery store, hardware store, school, auto shop, gas station.

When I was still a foolish kid, I believed the only way my book and I could flourish—truly live—was to leave. The plan was to find somewhere with more space, where people could explore and question and dream. I learned quickly how hungry the hard, cracked earth yearns for your feet the more you try to fly. Within a year, my English major felt like the joke my classmates said it was, and my book was stuffed into a box under old sweaters and junk.

Every time I stumbled upon it an immense pressure bloomed in my chest. Or rather, I became acutely aware of the way the air suffocated me. Then, for days, nothing in my life felt real. From my new business major to the button-upped friends that came with it.

So lost in my thoughts, I almost miss the small carving on a tree along the trail.

It wasn't a special tree for most of its life. Tall, thin, and gray-brown like all the others. Then one day a boy came sprinting down the slope, a look of pure wonder in his eyes, his mouth gaped open. He skidded to a halt and pulled a small blade from his pocket which he used to carve excitedly into the nearest tree.

A series of half circles connecting at their tips until they form a cloud.

I brush my hand over the dulled grooves before continuing up the last few feet of the slope to the cliff edge at the top. Tingles vibrate through me like the stark plucks of guitar strings. A low, almost melancholy note sounds in my head. It rises and rises in pitch until I'm only inches from the brink.

A sea of ink black treetops spreads out below me, the town diminished to a handful of smothered white lights. A hellish parallel to the cloud-filled sky above.

I'm not ready to look up.

It always started when my eyes met the skies.

Foolishness creeps in, drowning out the song. I'm a grown man who snuck out in the dead of night to traipse through the woods. To look for fairies.

My gut twists at the word, and I take a step back. The world almost seems to darken as I do.

What if I imagined everything? What if I wasted my childhood up here, drawing and dreaming?

The boy who carved a cloud into the tree steps into the clearing next to me. Large brown eyes gaze upwards at the stars, and he smiles. I haven't seen that smile in so long. My eyes prick with hot tears. He steps closer to the ledge. Though he doesn't look back, I know he wants me to join him.

I come to his side, the way he's always come to mine.

I look up to the sky.

Stillness comes first. An unsurety in the air, as if the cliff hasn't yet decided who I am.

Then.

Melted sherbet spills across the dark sky, starting off pastel and soft, then boldening into tangerine, lavender, and dusky rose. The stars brighten and twinkle amidst the burst of color. The trees below sink deeper into darkness in contrast.

I don't want to look away. The colors are even brighter than I remember.

But I can't miss her.

A flickering light from below catches my eye. As if an invisible hand slowly lifts a candle, its delicate flame dancing, a warm light rises.

Within that light, is a woman.

My hands clasp over my mouth, caging in the gasp, or shout, or maybe even scream building in my throat.

She's here. She's really here.

Her brown skin catches the light with a golden shimmer. Waist-length black hair flows behind her, caught in the breeze of her ascension. Large dark eyes look upwards, and only upwards.

She is not a fairy. Fairies aren't real. This is real. This is happening. I am here with the girl I watched all those many nights ago fly up from the forest into the sky. Every night, without fail, she would make her voyage. There were many mornings I would race here before school, hoping to see her descend, but she never did.

Wrapped in light, her body leans forward slightly, one arm raised up, the other down and outwards like wing. She's halfway there now.

My fingers itch to wrap around a pencil. To capture this moment on another blank page of my book.

I lower myself to the ground clumsily, never taking my eyes off her. She's close enough that if I shout she may hear me, but far enough that trying would feel ridiculous. Not that I hadn't tried before. I've screamed, waved my hands, even shot a flare gun once.

She never looked at me. But that's okay. Because I can see her, I know she exists.

The sherbet edges begin to roll back in as she nears the clouds. My heart clenches with each disappearing inch. Sooner than I'm ready, the colors take her, and the sky in turn devours them until I'm left with the dark navy of normalcy.

I cry for the first time in years. Not the chugging, chest wrenching, dry-heaving sob of someone with their back against a wall. Not the raw throated wail of an abused heart. I cry the surrendered and terrified tears of a dream realized.

Every morning my alarm goes off and I'm immediately reminded I'm sleeping in a twin-sized child's bed. My cold feet dangle off the edge, the nightstand juts into my shoulders, the scuffed headboard leaves chips of maroon paint on my scalp.

Still, I rise with a smile.

Inches away, sprawled across an old desk marked up and down with colored pencil lines and stickers are the pages of my book. For the past week after returning from the cliff edge, I've stayed up until the early morning pouring over my drawings.

Last night I dug through boxes in my closet, sifting through novelty tees and plain hoodies, and found more notebooks. My special book was a gift from my grandmother the year she learned I liked to draw. Its where my hopes were kept. But these notebooks, filled end to end with stories and ramblings, are where I planned my way to them.

I discovered I never named her, but I did imagine she was a warrior angel. Or a fallen star who had to find her way back home every night. Or the embodiment of light. *What if all light had the potential to become human if it burned bright enough?* I asked the pages.

The creak of a chair in the living area yanks me from her.

Even behind the locked door of my room, and the thickness of my skull, I feel like Dad knows what I'm thinking about. And he—they—anyone who knows—will poison us with their judgement.

"I need to go to the store today," Dad says loud enough for me to hear.

He won't admit it, but he needs help with his shopping. Just like he needs help cleaning, cooking, sometimes even moving about the house.

I sigh, prepare myself, then leave my room to face the day. As long as I can see her tonight, I can bear it. "Sure. Have you thought any more about getting a home nurse?" Might as well start that argument early.

"I," *cough, hack,* "don't need," *cough, cough,* "any help."

"No, you don't *want* any help, but you do need it."

He waves his hand at me. Even in the short time I've been here, his energy has depleted. Yelling used to be his weapon of choice. Now he only grunts and gestures.

"I'll get dressed and head to the store, you stay here. Think about what you need and give me a list."

When I turn my back, he exhales deeply. Something about it tugs at my heart. It sounds weighted, like the kind of breath that plummets to the floor, taking you with it.

That weight presses upon my shoulders as I slip on a clean shirt and the same pair of jeans I've been wearing every day. When I'm back in the living room, I find Dad asleep in his chair. His face is still, the sagging skin like carved stone. His chest rises—wait, no it isn't.

I dash forward, my heavy boots shaking the floorboards and walls.

"Dad? Dad?" I go to shake him but remember at the last second how fragile he is. Instead, I cup his face. His skin feels like cold cut meat. I tap him lightly with both hands.

My eyes rove over every feature, looking for movement.

Just when the silence gets so thick it feels like cotton shoved into my ears, his eyes flutter open. They're brown like mine. Shaped similarly too. If not for my mother's flatter nose and thick eyebrows, this is my aged and weary face.

"The fuck are you lookin' at?"

I jump back, hands flying into my pockets. Then I scowl. "Thought you died or something."

He wheezes into a dirty hand towel. One I've had to rip from his hands to clean for him. "Well, I didn'. I need milk, eggs, batteries for the remote, orange juice, bacon…"

I scramble to type all this in my phone as he continues to bark out items. Twenty items later, seven of which he's not allowed to have according to his doctor, I'm stomping across the front yard towards town.

So far, I haven't needed to venture any farther than the overgrown front lawn, but I knew sooner or later the time would come. There's only one road to follow towards the main strip and its barely wide enough for two cars. Memories of clenching, every time another pick-up going as fast as Dad's would fly by us, accompany me until the tops of sun-bleached roofs begin to peek out from the surrounding pines.

The closer I get, the more the familiar buildings of "downtown" reveal themselves. And the more I shrivel up like a raisin. It's before this peanut gallery that the other boys would spot me and follow until out of view of the adults, planning their insults. They probably could have accosted me right in front of the church with the way everyone felt about me—the boy who believes in faeries.

But I am not a little boy anymore. And turns out…they are all wrong. The corners of my mouth curl upwards. Then they plummet back to where they belong when I step onto a half-submerged sidewalk, announcing I've arrived.

The sidewalk takes me past a couple new coffee shops, the library where I checked out every fantasy book it had, and the town hall where the most brutal school dances were held. A few eyes catch mine, but I pass before recognition dawns on them.

Embarrassment creeps up the back of my neck when I realize I'm practically power walking. I'm still running from their judgement and the shame it inspires.

Spotting the grocery store ahead, I lower my eyes to the ground until I pass through its doorway.

To my luck, it's mostly empty.

Shopping takes all of ten minutes to do. There are only seven double-sided shelves and a third of the items on the list aren't here. At least they have the batteries. I wouldn't dare return to

Dad without them. If he's sucked into the T.V., he's not talking to me.

After slapping the groceries down on the conveyor belt, I grab a small bag of gummy candy for myself. The clerk keeps glancing up at me out of the corner of her eye. Her name is Shelby, she used to work at the Post Office. For one horrifying month she dated Dad long after my mother split. She was witness to many fights about my "weird shit."

Knowing it's coming, I reach around her to grab a couple plastic bags and start tossing everything in myself. I pay, she hands me a receipt.

"Hey are you—?"

"No." I grab the bags and leave. Another text to add to the community chat. Tyler's son is indeed home, and he's just as weird as he ever was. I hope they find me rude and unapproachable. The opposite of the soft target I used to be.

The trip back to the house feels as if it takes half the time. Probably because I'm just shy of jogging.

Somehow Dad and I have managed to fend for ourselves for food so far. There's always been a box of bars or some stale cereal to plug the holes of hunger. But tonight, we need to cook. I offer to make spaghetti because it will take me twenty minutes, we'll cram it down our throats in three, then retreat to our separate spaces.

Water, noodles, salt.

No oregano, no basil, no parmesan cheese, just salt and pepper.

I dump the canned red sauce over the steaming noodles and bring two heaping plates to the small kitchen table.

"What do you want to drink?" I ask.

He says, "A beer."

I bring him a glass of water because he can't have beer. The look he gives makes me wonder if he'll smack the glass out of my hands. He takes it with a grumble.

We sit across from each other, the salt and pepper between us. The forking of the food into our mouths commences. We're almost there. Just a few more bites and I can clear the table, yawn, and vanish.

"You didn' learn to cook with all that money you made from that fancy job?" Dad muffles through a mouth of noodles.

Bastard. Why? We were so close.

"I worked ten hours a day, and they didn't pay me that well. Anyway, you're welcome for making dinner," I gripe.

"Your mother couldn' cook either. No one in this family can."

"Mmm."

"If they're workin' you so hard, I'm surprised they let you come down here for a month."

I really don't want to talk about this.

"Yeah, well, they did."

"Seems suspicious is all. Think you'll even have a job when you go back? Those corporate assholes will fire anyone for anythin'."

"Maybe. I don't know." Jesus.

"You don' know? Seems like somethin' you should know."

My hands slam down on the table. I don't even realize until the plates clink against the linoleum. "Don't worry about it, Dad."

He doesn't miss a beat. "I do worry about it. You need to have a job. You need to be makin' money and buildin' a life."

I look down at my lap, expecting to see the plaid of my jacket, my worn jeans, peeks of my heavy boots. What greets me is scrawny legs bouncing uncontrollably in ill-fitting shorts, and a tee shirt with a faded soda logo.

"I'm not ten, you don't get to lecture me. *Drop it.*"

"Oh, but I do. I saw those drawins'. You may as well be ten if you're still doin' that weird shit. What if your job found out you like to draw faeries, they would definitely fire you then." His eyes open wide. "They *did* fire you didn' they? That's why you called out of the blue after almost a decade of not hearin' from you. They found out what you like to do and decided they didn' want a child working for 'em."

This time I slam my hands deliberately. He flinches, and a part of me lights up. I feel taller and wider, filling up the tiny kitchen like a mutating shadow. "Actually, I quit. And no, they didn't find me drawing *faeries*. I left because it was a shit job doing shit work that made me feel like my existence was a windowless gray room." His mouth opens to rebuttal. I shut him down. "It's none of your fucking business what I do with my life. It wasn't back then and it sure as hell isn't now."

That's the end of that. I'm clearly the stronger one here. When I say it's over, it's over.

"So, what are you gonna do then, huh? Hang out on my couch until you're old like me? Spend your days complainin' about how hard life is then go sneak into the woods at night?"

Just like that, I'm small again.

"Yeah, I know what you've been doin'," he continues. "I may be sick, but I can still hear you comin' and goin'. When are you gonna grow up?"

By now my hands have abandoned dinner entirely and curled into white fists. I'm scrambling to figure out how to release this hot, explosive energy growing inside me, but every idea melts from the heat. I can't think of anything to say. I'm just…angry. More than that, I'm humiliated. Ashamed. I found her again, proving to myself that she is real, and he wants to take that away from me again.

"I'm going to bed," I manage to gurgle out.

"Sit down!" he has the audacity to order. Which I ignore.

"You're wastin' your time on this nonsense. You need to accept reality and grow the hell up. Go back to the city, get your job back and leave that fuckin' fairy book here. They'll never look at you no matter how many nights you spend on that ledge," he shouts to my retreating back.

I've slammed my room door and flopped down on my bed before it hits me. In seconds, I'm back on my feet and racing to the kitchen.

When I find my father, he's leaning wearily against the counter, attempting to scrub red sauce off the plates. I rip the plate from his hand, and it clatters against the metal sink with a sharpness that rings in my ears.

"What the hell do you mean they'll never look at me?"

"That's not what I meant to say. I meant—I meant..." His hands scramble for the plate again as if washing those chunks of tomato down the drain is the most important task in the world.

"No. Don't you fucking do that. What do you mean?"

He abandons the dishes and tries to duck around me towards the living room, but I step in his path.

"Get out of my damn way," he demands.

"No." I cross my arms.

He throws his hands up in frustration. "You misheard me, I don' know nothin' about your fuckin' faeries. Maybe you should just leave tomorrow, I don' need or want you here, alright?"

He tries to move past me again.

Something inside me bursts forth. Something long buried under a lifetime's worth of fears and worries. It looks like pale light, floating among swaths of lavender, rose, and tangerine. It feels like hope.

I rest my hand gingerly on his shoulder, swallow the pride clogging my throat, and plead. *"Please."*

Incoherent mumbles leak from his lips. His eyes dodge mine. He grips his chin, pulling the skin. Finally, he says, with a tremor in his voice, "I—I've seen 'em."

I'm sitting down, I think. My legs are suddenly against something hard, I'm looking up at my father. I must be sitting. The three words echo in my head.

I've. Seen. Them.

He stands before me, his entire body hunched over, wearing a weighted blanket of shame I recognize as the one I left here in Trickle before I left.

"But you don't believe in *faeries*," I stammer.

"They're not faeries."

They? There's more than one?

Two urges wage a war inside me. One wishes to shoot up from the chair and launch into a tirade about the pain he's caused, the years wasted believing I was alone in this. The other wants me to hold my breath, terrified even the slightest wrong move will send Dad into a backtracking tailspin.

To my shock, Dad slowly lowers down into the chair next to me. "I don' know what they are. Your grandma didn' know either. Neither did her sister or their grandpa before that." He takes a deep breath that reminds me of an old car struggling to start. "It's called The Sight, and it's a curse in our family."

"The Sight…" I mimic.

"Yea. We can see 'em. Them, uh, people of the sky. Mom told me they come down durin' the day to experience the earth, absorb the essence of the flowers or some shit. Then they return to their world above the clouds at night."

"Are they human?"

"I don' think so. They're somethin' different. Magic." He nearly chokes on the last word. As if he's trying to swallow his own tongue to keep it from speaking.

"So, I'm not crazy."

"No, son. You're cursed."

I sputter. Cursed? This is the greatest moment of my life. Shame lifts off me like a suit of armor is being removed, plate by useless plate. "This is not a curse, Dad. This is incredible. Why didn't you tell me? Why did you—" My brows furrow at memories of his red, swollen face screaming, spit flying and cigarette ash dropping to the carpet. The layers of disgust in his voice.

Something tells me the same memories invade him too when his eyes find the floor. "I was trying to protect you from disappointment. See, I did what you did. Spent too much of my life, up until I met your mother even, goin' to that ledge. I watched one of 'em, a boy, fly into the sky every night. When mom found out she told me the same thing I'm tellin' you now." When he looks at me, his eyes are glazed over with moisture. "Let it go. Or you'll waste your life chasin' somethin' that will never truly feel real."

I make to argue, but Dad doubles over, his hand clutching his chest. His eyes bug out, jaw tightening. A coughing fit like nothing I've heard before follows. I rush to the living area for his hand towel, then refill his glass of water. Then I place an unsure hand on his back and lightly pat because I don't know what else to do.

"Yeah, that's helpin'," he manages between hacks.

I scoff but change my taps to soft circles.

My heart tightens as his episode subsides. He reaches for the water with a shaky arm and takes small sips. The rag is covered in dark brown gunk.

We look at it, both of us understanding.

"Do you want to come with me tonight?" It's out before my brain registers that I want to ask.

He responds with an incredulous look, but doesn't say no.

"I can' make it up that slope anymore…barely get to the couch from here."

Still not a no.

"And I'm tired," he adds.

"How about I wake you up in few hours, and we give it a try? We can take as much time as we need," I offer.

He argues. He grumbles. He scolds me for not listening to his warning. He swears it's a waste of time, even when he admits to trying a few years ago before he got sick, just to see.

He never says no.

I help him into his bed and tell him I'll wake him in a few hours.

My hand hovers over the book.

A backpack sits on the desktop, wide open. Inside are several clean rags, water bottles, my father's inhaler, some other medication, and a flare gun. There's still room for one more thing.

I just can't bring it. All it would lead to is drawings. Drawings would lead to stories. Stories would lead to dreams. Inevitably, dreams would lead to reality.

Decided, I zip up the backpack and fling it over my shoulder, then turn to leave the room. Dad waits for me in his chair in front of the TV. He argued from the moment I woke him to getting him dressed and in his chair to waiting while I packed.

"Are you ready?" I ask, giving him one last chance to back out. A part of me hopes he does, as embarrassment swoops in at the thought of sharing this with him. That ledge being tainted with his misery and judgment sends a punch to my gut.

"Yea, let's get this over with." He sluggishly pulls on a pair of hiking boots before reaching for two walking sticks that I leaned against his chair.

Then we're heading for the door. I feel a tug on my backpack. When I twist my neck, my father is patting it like he's looking for something.

"What?" I accuse.

"You're not bringin' it?"

We both know what "it" is. Embarrassment continues to thicken the air. This might be a mistake.

"No." Before Dad can respond I've stepped onto the porch, but he doesn't follow. He's hobbled back across the living room to rustle around the shelves against the wall for who knows what. When he's found whatever it is, he joins me outside.

A whistling Autumn wind kicks up leaves and twigs, skittering them across our path as we make our way around the house. I follow Dad instead of leading after he trips over the first two pieces of junk in his path. When we reach the forest, I walk beside him, a hand hovering behind his arm. He barks it away several times until I relax enough to give him some space.

We move slowly, taking frequent breaks for coughing fits, water, and bickering. To pass the time I ask every question that pops into my head about The Sight. Where does it come from? Is it witchcraft? Some kind of mental disorder? Is it only in our family? Do others have it? Is it something I can Google?

He has no answers, and he quickly annoys at my prying.

The moon has drifted halfway across the sky by the time I spot the cloud carving. I don't think I've ever been so nervous.

Dad pauses just before the ground begins to level out. The clearing sprawls out before us. A strange sadness crawls into his eyes as he looks towards it. When he notices I'm watching, he grunts and carries on. Together, we amble up to the cliff edge and look out over the miles of forest below and navy, cloudy sky above.

The silence between us and the trees is crisp as the air. I want to look for her, but all I can do is watch dad's eyes rove endlessly around in earnest.

Minutes tick by and the sky remains dark. His brows drop lower and lower, mouth tightening into a thin line. Without a word he turns abruptly and starts marching back towards the slope, his face noticeably red even in the dark.

"Dad!" I exclaim. When he whips around, the flourishing colors are reflected in his wide eyes. He rushes back to the edge, using my arm to steady himself when he stops. We watch the sky change; the colors leaking out amongst the clouds.

And then, two lights like fallen stars begin to float their way up.

Dad's mouth drops open. His trembling hands squeeze my arm. "It's him," he gasps.

I see my girl, arms spread wide, legs pointed, flying. Beside her is a man, wrapped in the same white light.

My heart swells. There really is a whole world of them up there. I wish I had my book to capture every thought and hope, every dream of this magical place and the people in it.

I feel something being crushed into my stomach. When I look down, I see Dad is thrusting a small legal pad and a pen into me.

"Quick!" he cries. "Draw this. I don' wanna forget."

My full heart bursts, filling every inch of me with this feeling. One I know will never truly leave me, that never has, no matter how much I tried to stuff it away under junk in old boxes.

I take the pen and paper and look outwards.

The first thing I'll draw is the look of pure wonder in their eyes as they lock onto ours.

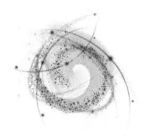

ABOUT THE AUTHOR

Darby Cox enjoys writing fantasy and literary fiction. She grew up in a military family where she moved around a lot. Didn't make many friends that way, but it helped her develop a great imagination and love of stories. She now lives in Philly with her anxious dog Milez.

RAINSTORM
BY
JUDITH PRATT

RAINSTORM

No one was going to stop for a soaking wet guy in work clothes. He'd get their leather seats all stained with water. And sweat.

The lawnmowing company had us working at daylight to get ahead of the rain and kept us at it until the rain actually started and the bus lines stopped. A buddy gave me a ride to a about four miles from my place. I can't afford to rent a motel, so I walked. At least the rain washed off some of the sweat and dirt.

Walking gave me too much time to worry about Jake. He and my ex-wife now live with her mother in a neighborhood full of gangs, with a lousy school. I send everything I can to him and Emily, but it's never enough. Jake wants better shoes, a computer, stuff kids need. I know because I never had it. When I was Jake's age, I read stories about kids who killed dragons, or got rich by inventing something amazing. But I stopped reading them because life never has happy endings. It doesn't even have endings. It just goes on and on and you do the best you can.

When the truck pulled up ahead of me, I was worrying so hard that I didn't even notice it at first. Then the driver opened the door and called, "Need a ride?" I jogged over, opened the door. "Thanks," I said.

The dash lights showed a youngish woman. A black knit cap covered her hair with a few reddish curls sticking out underneath. She had a wide mouth and a snub nose. The inside of the car was too dark to tell any more about her.

"Not a great day for a hike," she said. "Where you headed?"

I gave her the address. "But anywhere near is fine," I said. "Just getting outa the rain is nice."

She said it wasn't a problem, that it was close to home for her. "I'm Sophy," she said. "We live in the woods outside of Muirtown."

"Mike," I told her. "Sorry to get your truck so wet."

"It's used to getting wet," she said.

I wiped rain off my face with the sweaty rag I usually tie around my head. It felt good to sit down. I'd already worked twelve hours. I run the weed whacker, because I don't chop down anyone's nice flower garden by accident like some of the other guys. It's a lot sweatier work than sitting on those giant mowers all day.

Living out in the country had seemed like a great idea at first. Got a cheap little shack on a back road that my buddy Rafe and I could afford. Drive to work in his old Nova. Make enough money working for rich people so I could send childcare payments for my son back in the city.

But now I was pissed at Rafe. He's always been a flake. He quit Barcello's Landscaping after only a couple months, got a job selling cars. "I don't need no skin cancer or heat stroke," he told me. His job isn't too far from mine, so at least I still had a ride. Not today, though. I'd called him to say I was working late, and he'd said he could pick me up, but he never showed. I'd called again as I was leaving work, but his phone had gone to voice mail.

In the truck, I found myself talking, telling Sophy about Rafe, and Barcello's, and how I'd had my own business back near the city but it collapsed in the bad times, and how my wife left, and about my son. I never talk about myself like that. I guessed that Sophy girl was a good listener, or something.

Before I realized how much I'd been talking, we were headed down toward my place near Freeville. I was just starting to wonder why I'd said so much when the truck slowed and stopped.

The bridge was out.

"What the hell," I said. We'd had plenty of rain this summer, and the bridge had always been fine. I had no idea how to get home any other way.

"Tell you what," Sophy said. "Come spend the night at our house. I'm going back to town in the morning and can take you to work."

I objected, of course, but she just laughed and reversed the truck, backing away from the dark rush of water, then K-turning in the narrow road to head back the way we'd come. I didn't want to have to sleep out in the rain, so I didn't argue any more.

After about five miles, we turned left. The truck bounced and splashed along a dirt road, then pulled around back of a big old house that even had a turret of some kind. Sophy rolled the truck into a barn. A couple of chickens squawked as we got out. Then Sophy led the way up slippery wooden steps to the back door.

The kitchen smelled so wonderful I almost drooled. Lunch had been a long time ago.

"This is Serena," Sophy said. The woman was tall, with long brown hair. Not old enough to be Sophy's mother

"Serena, this is Mike. I gave him a ride. The Ludlow bridge into Freeville is out, so he couldn't get home."

"How annoying for you," Serena said, smiling. "Welcome. Supper will be ready soon. Sophy, maybe you can find Mike some dry clothes."

Sophy led me down a narrow, white-painted hall and up a few stairs. "You can wash up here," she told me. "Hand me out your wet clothes. Some of Serena's stuff might fit you. I'll get 'em."

The bathroom had a bunch of towels rolled up in an open cabinet, and a big bar of plain soap, but no shower. While I was getting as clean as I could manage without a shower, Sophy knocked, and handed some sweat clothes through the door. They were a little tight, but baggy enough to cover me. She also gave me clean socks. I'd already shed my soggy boots at the door.

Dressed, I padded out into the hall in my stocking feet and paused. Had we come up some stairs? Where were they? The whole place smelled like chicken stew and fresh bread, so following my nose wasn't going to lead me back to the kitchen

Sophy came clattering down some stairs I hadn't seen before, red curls bouncing. "Come on, let's eat."

I followed her down a hall to some more stairs, down another hall, and into the kitchen. A medium-sized man, with short gray-brown hair and olive-pale skin, stood up from the table. "Sam, this is Mike," said Sophy. "Did Serena tell you about the bridge?" Sam nodded but didn't put out his hand. I wouldn't think much of my daughter, or sister, bringing home some stranger either.

For the next half hour, eating took up most of my attention. Apple pie followed the stew and bread. I tried to mind my manners, but it was hard work. I was pretty hungry and hadn't had such good food since Emily left me. The other three talked about the rain, and their chickens, and Sophy's work, which had something to do with the ocean. I mow a lot of lawns for the big houses along the ocean, but Sophy worked in in a town called Maireport. I'd never been there.

"Time for bed," Serena said. I was embarrassed. I'd been nodding off over my pie.

Sophy led me to a small bedroom, either up or down some stairs. I was asleep before I hit the pillow.

Sun in my eyes woke me up. I jumped out of bed, thinking I was late. Then I realized that I wasn't at home. If I was going to be late to work, there was nothing I could do about it. Calling would just give the boss a chance to yell at me. I put Serena's clothes back on and went hunting for a bathroom with a shower. I didn't find one. Instead, I ended up in the hallway that led to the kitchen. This was one confusing house.

I stopped in the doorway. Serena was sitting at the table, writing something. My stocking feet hadn't made a sound, but she turned and smiled at me. "You'd probably like a shower," she said. "We washed your clothes; they're drying. Come on, I'll show you the bathroom. I'll toss your clothes in when they're dry." Head spinning, I followed her through the confusing house to another bathroom. This one had a big old-fashioned bathtub, with a shower rigged over it.

Cleaned up and mostly respectable, I actually found my way back to the kitchen, although I have no idea how I did it. Nothing looked like it had last night.

In the kitchen, Serena was gone, and Sophy sat at the table with Sam. A calico cat curled in a big bay window. Its face was half white and half calico brown. I heard chickens clucking around outside.

As I entered, Sam stood up. "Serena's getting eggs for our breakfast," he said.

No. She. Sam was a she. I could see the curve of small breasts under her tee shirt. Maybe the confusing house was getting to me.

"Sophy and I are having coffee and rolls," Sam said. "You drink coffee?" Wordless, I nodded, and Sam got down a mug, filled it, joined us at the table.

I'd missed it, that Sam was a woman. Because of the name, I guess. She hadn't changed; I'd just been stupid. My face got hot. Were Sam and Serena a couple? They hadn't acted all that affectionate last night. But given how tired I was, they could have done it under the table and I wouldn't have noticed.

Serena came in with a basket of eggs, like we were living in another century, and proceeded to turn them into a cheese omelet. Breakfast for me was usually a donut, washed down by coffee in a cardboard cup. Here, the coffee came in one of those chunky white mugs and tasted terrific. So did the omelet.

After breakfast, I thanked Serena and Sam as well as I could, with Sophy calling, "Hurry up, Mike, we'll be late!" from the back steps.

As we drove toward town, Sophy said, "If you'd rather live closer to work, I know someone who might have a room you could rent. Just a bed and a microwave, but no more hikes in the rain."

It sounded good to me. I'd finally got hold of Rafe this morning while I was getting dressed. He was all apologetic. Some of the guys had gone out for drinks, the bar was loud, he hadn't heard the phone. He hadn't been back home either; he'd stayed with one of the guys. I wondered if the bridge was still out.

I even wondered if it had ever really been out.

I just told Rafe, "Okay, man," and hung up on him. He owed me two months' rent. Our deal was not working.

To my surprise, the boss didn't complain about me being late. He usually hollers at anyone who gets there even three minutes after seven.

After work, I got on a bus and went to the address Sophy had given me. Mrs. Jackson was a small, round lady, who lived in a little ranch-style house in a run-down neighborhood. The house needed paint, but the tiny yard was neatly kept. Inside, the place was as clean as my Aunt Patricia's house, and that's saying something.

Mrs. Jackson showed me a room with a bed, a table, and a corner with a kitchen counter, a microwave, and one of those under-the-counter refrigerators. It had a window looking out on the side of the house next door.

"My last tenant just moved out," she told me. "Went into business for herself."

The price was less than I paid for the house I shared with Rafe. "It's great," I told her. "I can give you references from my landscaping job."

"If that Sophy child says you're okay, you're okay. She sends me most of my tenants. Got a rental agreement for you to sign." And she marched into the hall—for a small lady, she moved fast. An Asian man was coming out of another room, and almost ran into her.

"I'm so sorry, Miz Jackson" he said. "I was just coming to see you. I'll be moving out next week. My new store is doing well, and I found a house for my wife and baby. They'll be joining me soon." He smiled at me and put out his hand. "Chi Nooyen," he said, only he didn't pronounce it exactly like that. I shook hands and said, "Mike Hanley."

Mrs. Jackson said, "I'll be downstairs. Come sign the agreement and get the key." And she charged off.

I must have looked worried, because Chi said, "She always sound curt, but she is wonderful landlady. Do you plan to live here?" When I nodded, he said, "My room has a better view. Come look."

This room looked out on a little back yard, with an ash tree and neat flowerbeds full of marigolds. "Thanks," I told Chi. "You're right about the view. Congrats on getting yourself a house."

"Everyone who rents rooms here does well," he said. "Kadeesha, who had the room you looked at, had been fired from her job in a big clothing store. She started designing her own dresses, and they are now most fashionable. She said this place is magic! I laughed at her, but my store has done so well, I think she may be right."

I thanked him again. We went downstairs together, and Mrs. Jackson agreed to let me have Chi's room. I signed the rental agreement and paid the first month's rent.

"Does Sophy ever come visit you?" I asked.

"Not often," said Mrs. Jackson. "She's got some job studying the ocean, down to Maireport. Once you're on your feet, I'll see her again, bringing me another tenant."

I took the room. Rafe complained, but I didn't care. Already I'm saving money. Jake got his computer and his shoes. Then Barcello made me a supervisor and raised my pay. In a few more years, I'll be able to buy a little house.

It's a happy ending, just like the stories I used to read. The magic is working.

I'm just not sure who the magic belongs to.

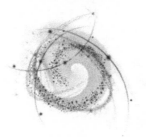

ABOUT THE AUTHOR

My varied experiences—actor, director, professor, fundraiser, and freelance writer—inspire my novels, stories, and plays. I began as a playwright. Then a story appeared that would not fit on a stage, so I wrote a novel, and another, and one and a half more. My novels in print are *The Dry Country* and *Siljeea Magic*. Short stories followed soon after. They appear in various magazines, online, and in actual print. Some of the characters in Rainstorm come from my first play, *Chimera*.

For more: www.judithpratt.com

I live in Ithaca, NY, with a husband and three loud cockatiels.

MELTING SNOW
BY
J.Z. WESTON

MELTING SNOW

Matt yawned as he reached into the kitchen cabinet to pull out a coffee pod. Instead of the plastic container he expected, his hand closed on a small metal object. He pulled it out and blinked at his dead wife's ring. Olivia had worn that ring every day of her life—or at least, every day that Matt had known her—until her fingers swelled up and rings were no longer an option. She'd worn her wedding bands on a chain when that happened, but this one had disappeared.

Matt turned the ring over in his hands, gazing at the reddish orange stone and tracing the angles and curves with a fingertip. He thought this had been a family heirloom, but he wasn't sure. He'd always assumed that he would get to hear the story again, that he'd have another chance to remember, but now he never would.

He closed his eyes, counted to ten, and pulled himself back together. He couldn't fall apart now. He needed to shovel the snow that fell last night, and for that, he needed coffee. But he couldn't put the ring down. A quick detour to the bedroom later, it hung from a chain around his neck, to rest against his sternum under the sweatshirt.

Now, coffee. He grabbed one of the French Vanilla pods Olivia had loved. She would wrap her hands around the mug and inhale deeply, savoring the aroma like it wasn't the crappiest coffee on earth. He caught his breath as the memory poked the fresh wound of loss, and he noticed only three of the French Vanilla remained in the box. He put his back and grabbed something else. He couldn't run out of her favorite coffee. Not yet.

His bare feet froze on the linoleum floor, and he shifted his weight to one side and the other as he waited for the machine to spit out a brown, coffee-like substance. When the last dribbles had emptied into his mug, he took a drink. He nearly gagged on the tepid liquid. Stupid machine was on the fritz again, and on one of the coldest mornings of the year. He longed for a hot beverage with his entire being, and the ring flashed hot against his chest. When he steeled himself to take another swallow, the coffee almost burned his mouth.

What the heck? Could the coffee have heated unevenly? Matt didn't have the energy to think about it too much. He emptied the mug and readied himself to assess the damage from the storm.

From his front stoop, he looked out at white and gray houses blended with fresh snow in the early morning light. At least a foot of dense snow blanketed every yard, more where the plows had banked it by the road. Matt was the first one out, so not even the sound of shoveling disturbed the silence. He grabbed a shovel and worked his way down the straight walkway from his house to the sidewalk. The snow was deep, but light, so the work went quickly. The meditative rhythm of stoop-shovel-lift-toss filled his mind, drowning out all thoughts of coffee, rings, or loss. He wished he could spend his whole day out there like that. He cleared one end of the sidewalk, then turned around to work his way towards the driveway.

The snowbank proved more difficult. The plow had compacted the snow into a solid mass, and he was soon sweating enough from the exertion that he had to unzip his coat.

The work of clearing the snow remained a welcome distraction until Matt went to clear his car off and saw he had forgotten to lift his windshield wipers last night. He hoped the snow would be powdery enough he could just wipe them clear, but no such luck. A thick layer of ice held his wipers prisoner. He grabbed the scraper from out of his car and started chipping away at the windshield, cursing his own forgetfulness and fantasizing about watching this mess melt away.

Heat flared against Matt's chest, and he stumbled as his scrapper slipped straight across the windshield. The ice flew off in a smooth sheet that landed in the snow with a *thunk*. Cold water trickled away from his windshield wipers, which were suddenly free.

This was not normal.

First the coffee, now this. And a ring that flashed hot each time. Matt started connecting the dots, but the picture they drew made no sense. It was a ridiculous thought, utterly impossible, wishful thinking born of too many late nights playing D&D.

There were no magic rings in real life. It had to be a strange coincidence, but he needed to test the theory, or he'd never be able to let it go.

Matt was still the only person disturbing the quiet morning, so nobody saw him carry his snow shovel to his neighbor's driveway. Carol was a sweet older woman who lived alone. It would be a public service to clear out the plow bank at the end of her driveway, right? He focused on the snow in front of him, and thought of warmth, of heat, of summer. The snow sparkled, unchanged. He closed his eyes and focused harder, calling up images of heat, of summer sunlight. Still no change. What had he been thinking about when he cleared off his windshield? He thought about melting, about ice softening into water and flowing away.

Another wave of heat hit him, this one a tsunami that started in his chest and expanded outward. The snowbank crumbled and collapsed in on itself, a stop-motion animation of spring thaw. Five minutes later, the end of Carol's driveway was wet, but free of snow. He panted with the effort, the satisfied exhaustion of a good run.

"What a wonderful surprise. Thank you, Matt."

He whirled around to see Carol standing on her front stoop, her tall frame bundled up in snow boots, purple coat, and a trinity of mismatched hat, scarf, and gloves. She stomped towards him through her unshoveled walkway.

"I thought I was getting an early start on things, but it looks like you've beat me to it! You've already cleared your driveway and started on mine—very generous of you." Her face creased into a grin.

Matt shrugged. "It's a beautiful morning, and I was feeling energetic."

She stepped closer, reaching out to put her hand on his arm. "Still, it's a big help. Why don't you come on inside? I'll make you some coffee to say thank you."

Matt shrank back to dodge her hand. "It was no trouble, really. And I've already had one cup this morning."

"Then tea, or cocoa. Just let me thank you properly."

"Really Carol, it's fine. I didn't even finish the driveway, just cleared out the bank from the snowplow." He took a few steps backwards, towards the safety of his own house. "Anyway, I should get started on work. You take care, though."

He scuttled back to the front door before she could say anything else and locked it behind him.

When Matt went out to check his mail later that day, he found a platter of chocolate chip cookies wrapped up by his front door. He glanced around, but of course the snow didn't have any answers for him, and the icy wind soon pushed him back inside.

He ducked under the ridiculous crystal chandelier in the dining room—Olivia always wanted him to replace it, but there was no point now, was there?—and shoved aside a pile of magazines and unread mail to make space for the cookies. Gloves, books, or trash covered all the chairs, so he took the attached envelope to the living room and flopped onto the ratty couch to open it. The card inside showed a pastoral winter scene. The glitter accents stuck to his hand, and he tried to wipe it off on his jeans to no avail. Inside the card, Carol's looping cursive said, "Thank you again for your assistance this morning. I hope these cookies can sweeten up your day!"

Carol meant well, but she could be pushy. She must have brought over a dozen casseroles in the weeks after Olivia died. Matt told her it wasn't necessary, but she kept showing up. It made an already difficult time that much more awkward. Every time she showed up with another tuna casserole in her yellow and white dish, it reminded him of his loss, and he would once again be consumed with the knowledge that Olivia wasn't in the next room, sitting on their beat-up old sofa, paging through her favorite novel or waiting to show him some pretty dice she found on-line for whatever D&D campaign they were playing that year. It hit him all over again, and for a moment he could hardly breathe for the pain of it. He needed to get a hold of himself. It had been six months. Past time to stop wallowing.

Matt forced himself to get up off the couch. He meant to go into the kitchen to figure out something for dinner, but then he took a detour to the plate of cookies. Just a quick snack before dinner. He took a bite—cold, but still delicious.

This whole day had been insane. He had an actual, honest to goodness magic ring. How had Olivia kept this a secret? He could never have hidden something this awesome from her, and it kind of hurt that she had. But he had to assume she'd had her reasons. Had she ever used its powers? Now that he thought about, his heating bill did seem a bit higher than normal this winter. He was tempted to go double check his records from last year, but the more he followed this line of thinking the worse he felt, so he shut it down.

The more interesting question was, what he was going to do with this magic ring now that he had it? Melting that bit of snow for Carol had felt great, at least until she came out and made things weird. The magic had left him exhilarated, alive in a way he hadn't felt in more than a year, and it would be selfish for him not to use this windfall to help other people, right?

Matt picked up the plate of cookies and returned to the living room. He deposited the cookies on the coffee table, balancing the plate on top of a pile of D&D sourcebooks that he hadn't had the heart to put away. After a nerve-wracking search, he found his phone wedged between the couch cushions and opened an app to take notes on all the ways that a heat amulet might help people, especially in the winter. Two text message notifications came in, but he swiped them aside, too absorbed in his task to allow distractions. By the time he ran out of ideas, the whole plate of cookies was gone. Not the most balanced dinner, but he would survive.

He finally checked the two texts. One was from his brother checking in on him and the other from Dave, inviting him to join their old gaming group for a one-shot the next night. Matt had stopped showing up after Olivia got sick and couldn't make it, and once she was gone... Well, it didn't get any easier. He couldn't face a session without watching her sketching their characters or writing weird limericks about them. He plugged his phone in to charge without responding to either.

Matt was halfway through an interminable video call with clients on the west coast the next day when the snow started up again. He half-assed his way through the rest of the meeting, constantly looking out the second-floor window to assess how much snow had piled up. How soon could he go out with his magic ring? This whole situation was a bizarre dream come true, the escape from reality he'd been looking for.

By the time five o'clock rolled around and he could extricate himself from work, a tidy amount of snow had accumulated on the sidewalks. The plows had passed through, but very few people had gotten around to shoveling yet.

Snow still fell in gentle flurries when Matt stepped outside, but not enough to undo his work. Nobody was out on his quiet street right now, but that could change at any moment, so he would need to be inconspicuous. Matt did not relish the prospect of trying to explain to some busybody why the snow was melting around him.

The brittle cold stung his face when he stepped outside, but the longer he worked, the more the ring warmed him. The snow was so powdery underfoot that melting it would do more harm than good—nobody would thank him for making them shovel heavy slush. Matt stopped at a cutout in the curb where the plow had piled compacted snow. Nobody ever shoveled those out. He looked left and right for bystanders, and then focused on melting a path so that someone in a wheelchair or pushing a stroller could safely cross the street.

He ambled through more side streets, focusing his heat on snowbanks and slick stairs. He stepped onto a frozen puddle, hidden under the powdery snow, and had to catch himself on a chain link fence. He melted that puddle and kept his eyes open for any more traps like that. Wouldn't want someone to slip and fall.

As he finished clearing the lake of ice that had formed around the bus stop closest to his house, Matt's feet were getting numb. He'd been at it for over an hour. The ring was no longer flaring hot against his chest and keeping him warm, but he'd been so wrapped up in the task that he didn't notice. He turned to head for home and stumbled. This time, he didn't catch himself. Pain flared through his left ankle, and he grimaced as he put weight on it. He limped toward home.

Matt turned the corner onto his own street feeling proud of himself, if exhausted. This outing took more out of him than he'd expected, but it was well worth it.

Carol waved from her front stoop as he passed. He waved back in a neighborly fashion and continued on towards home.

"Matt!" She gestured for him to come over. Maybe he could pretend not to see her? He was too cold and tired to deal with this. But that would be rude, so he turned toward her house.

Carol smiled at him. "Isn't the sky just beautiful tonight?"

He looked around and realized that, yes, night had fallen while he was out there. A half-full moon slipped out from the clouds, but the only real illumination came from streetlights. He supposed it could be starkly beautiful, to the right eyes.

"Bit cold," he ventured, rubbing his numb hands together for emphasis.

"Oh no! I love the cold. There's no such things as bad weather, just inappropriate clothing." She smiled and wagged a finger at him. "Don't think I didn't notice you clearing the sidewalk, young man. Let me make you some dinner."

"Oh no, I wouldn't want to intrude." He started backing up to his house, desperate to escape this conversation.

"Are you sure? You can't eat takeout every night."

He did not eat takeout every night. Maybe more nights than he ought to, but his eating habits were none of her business.

"Thank you, but I actually have some ground meat defrosting that I need to use up. Maybe another time?"

She didn't push further, and Matt fled back to his house.

He trudged through the pit of discarded wrappers and dirty socks that was once his living room. A moment of shame stabbed at him. He needed to do something about it, but not tonight. Now he wished that he really did have ground beef. Hamburgers sounded amazing. He would have ordered a pizza, but he told Carol that he was cooking for himself, and he didn't want to be a liar.

He rummaged through the kitchen. Pasta, but no sauce. Cereal, but no milk. Hamburger buns, but not a patty to be found. Shredded cheese and canned beans, but no rice. He had plenty of food, but nothing that could be called a meal. Finally, he dug up a frozen burrito.

He grabbed a beer while his dinner went round and round in the microwave, figuring he'd earned it after all that work.

His phone chirped, and Matt pulled it out of his pocket to find a text from Dave, asking if he was going to make it to the one-shot tonight. Damn it, he had forgotten about that. The microwave beeped at him to pick up his burrito, and he texted Dave back with an excuse.

Matt took a bite of molten burrito. The cold middle turned his stomach, but by the time he reached the other end, it had cooled to a reasonable temperature, so dinner finished on a decent note.

His ankle was still throbbing, so he grabbed an ice pack and elevated it then queued up some made-for-streaming superhero movie. Within the hour, his phone chimed with email. He glanced at the notification—the movie was doing a slow pan of the jungle, so he didn't have to pay close attention—and saw it was from Dave. Matt considered ignoring it, but he felt guilty about skipping the gaming session, so he paused the movie. Dave had written a lengthy missive about how he was worried about him, and how it's not good to be this isolated for so long, and how people need people. He even made an awkward reference to Anakin Skywalker, before closing off with a joke about how adventurers need teams, and nobody ever defeated a dragon by themselves, so Matt had better come back to the game soon.

The whole thing was in bad taste, and absolute garbage to boot. Life wasn't a role-playing game. If the last two days had shown Matt anything, it was that magic really could be wielded to good use by one person, alone.

Matt resumed his superhero movie. He was doing fine.

Matt had never complained about a clear winter day before now. He limped through almost a week of sunny weather before the cold returned. He couldn't focus on work, could barely focus on TV. Every time he felt the ring against his chest he thought of Olivia, and it became more and more difficult to think about anything but her smile, her laugh, how she would have reacted to this TV show or that commercial.

It hurt. All he could do was fantasize about the moment when he would get to feel the rush of magic again. He tried using it to heat his coffee, or cook his food, or even warm up the house, but none of that gave him the sense of euphoria he'd gotten from his work outside.

So, the prediction of freezing rain came as a relief. Freezing rain meant slippery streets and sidewalks. Screw Dave and his advice—Matt knew he could be a hero all on his own. He set his alarm for 4:30am, to give himself plenty of time to work before the morning commute started. At the first blast of the alarm, Matt leapt out of bed. He threw on a sweatshirt and sweatpants, topped it with his winter coat, and rushed out the door to make the streets and walkways safe before people started heading to work.

At first he tiptoed along the sidewalks but quickly realized that he was not slipping. Apparently, he'd gotten good enough at this that the amulet melted the ice under his feet. He could move faster and cover more ground, even if his ankle still twinged when he stepped the wrong way. He crept down garden paths to front doors, de-icing stairs under the cover of darkness. He became a helpful ninja, a rogue who stole ice instead of gold as he dodged motion activated lights.

The ice turned to rain, but he kept going. Wet ice was even more dangerous, and it wouldn't be warm enough to melt on its own for hours. The rain soaked into his coat and jeans, plastering his hair down and seeping into the tops of his boots. Sure, it got a little cold, but the amulet would warm him back up in no time.

Matt carefully unlatched the gate to the next house, but a Jack Russell terrier pushed past his legs and raced down the street.

Shit.

He cursed the bastards who left their dog outside overnight in this weather and took off after it. The terrier cut through yards and plowed through icy intersections. Matt wondered how it was getting purchase on these slick streets. If Matt hadn't had his amulet, he'd barely have been able to walk, but with its help he was running at top speed to catch an idiot dog, ignoring the throbbing in his ankle. His heart pounded and throat burned with every gasp of air.

Finally—finally!—the little dog trapped itself between a garbage can and a chain link fence, and Matt managed to grab it. The dog, of course, squirmed and barked, desperate to get out of his grasp.

He regretted his moment of sympathy for the dog. He was exhausted from the run, his ankle was burning, and trying to de-ice the sidewalks while also managing to not drop a squirming, irritated canine was next to impossible. He supposed he should be grateful that the dog hadn't bit him yet.

It took far too long, but Matt eventually got the dog back to its home. He unlatched the gate with one hand, set the dog down and slammed the gate shut again in one motion. It was still barking its head off as he walked away, but it wasn't his problem anymore.

Now that he was no longer holding a dog, Matt started shivering. His feet felt like bricks, and he could barely flex his bare fingers. It was time to head home, even if he hadn't managed to de-ice every house and sidewalk. His feet moved on autopilot, while his mind drifted in a fog. He tucked his hands under his armpits to try to warm them up, but his coat was too wet to hold any heat.

A fog settled over his mind, and he started to slow down. He focused on the ring, tried to use it to heat up his coat, steam off some of this water, warm himself up. Nothing happened. The ring lay like ice against his chest, and no matter how hard he thought about warmth and fire and sunlight, he and the ring remained icicles.

Oh well. Nothing for it but to keep going. But he didn't recognize his surroundings. He must have taken a wrong turn somewhere in his exhaustion, and now all the houses looked the same, and the street signs blurred together. He stumbled in a haze, distracted by spots that needed his help—locks and stairs and driveways and car doors and a thousand iced-over details.

But he was lost. Hopelessly lost. He stumbled over to a covered bus stop and collapsed onto the bench inside. He just needed to rest. Just for a minute. Then he'd start looking for home again. Just a minute. He leaned against the glass wall and closed his eyes.

Next thing he knew, a hand was shaking his shoulder, and someone called his name.

Matt looked up to see Carol, holding an umbrella in her free hand.

"C'mon. Let's get you inside." She helped him get up and led him away. His field of awareness narrowed to her hand on his arm guiding him, and her voice muttering reassurances.

They arrived at her house. Matt stepped inside, and the heat almost overpowered him. How could anybody breathe in this hot house jungle? He started to drift towards the couch, but she steered him into her bathroom. "No upholstery until you've dried off."

She helped him out of his coat, which he now saw was dripping on her floor. She left him alone for a minute, and came back with a t-shirt, sweatpants, and a robe.

"I trust you're able to undress yourself and put these on?"

He nodded.

"When you're decent again, come into the kitchen. And if I don't see you in five minutes, I'm coming back to check on you, decent or not. You understand?" She closed the door without waiting for him to respond.

He fumbled with the buttons, but eventually got out of his wet clothes and into the dry ones Carol provided. The robe felt like it had just come from the dryer.

Matt held onto the pale-yellow stucco wall as he made his way through a formal dining room and into the kitchen. She handed him a steaming mug and gestured to a chair at her kitchen table, then settled across from him after he sat down.

He took a sip from the mug. Hot chocolate. He drained it in three more swallows. Carol refilled it, and he looked up at her with gratitude. He felt a little more human, a little more capable of thought.

"How did you find me?"

Carol glanced to the side. "I saw you leave over an hour ago, and when you never came back, I got worried.

Matt put his mug down. "You've been watching me?"

"I'm an early riser." After a lengthy pause, she continued. "I just want to help."

"You don't have to worry about me. I'm fine." Jesus Christ, why did everybody think he needed help?

Carol reached across the table and placed her hand on his. "It was hard when my Peter died. I didn't want to go out, didn't want to talk to anyone, didn't want to be reminded that the world kept spinning. It took a lot of people a lot of effort to bring me back from that. It's okay to need help."

Matt pulled his hand back. "Seriously, I'm fine."

"Oh? So, you weren't on the verge of hypothermia on a bench half an hour ago? You could have died out there!"

"Maybe I should have!" he shouted. "Then I'd be with her again."

Matt's knee banged against the table as he stood up. He wanted to scream. He wanted to throw this mug of hot chocolate against the wall and watch it shatter. He wanted to punch something, anything. But he wouldn't. Instead, he took deep, shuddering breathes, willing himself back to a state of calm. He put his hands on the table, leaning against it as he shook from something other than the cold.

"I don't— I didn't mean—" He couldn't bring himself to finish.

Carol looked at him, that same compassionate expression on her face.

Matt lowered himself back into his seat. "I'm sorry for getting upset."

"You lost your wife. It would be stranger if you didn't get upset sometimes."

"I admit, things got out of hand today, but it won't happen again."

"Matthew," Carol said his name as gently as she might cup a baby bird. "You're a good person. I see you out there clearing everyone's sidewalks, though I don't know where you're getting that much salt. You care about other people… Please, you don't have to carry this all alone."

"But I do. I'm the one who has to find a way to live with this pain. Nobody else can do that for me."

"That's not true. Please, talk to someone. If not me, then someone. It'll help, I promise you."

"Maybe." He wished that he could promise her more—she'd been so kind to him today—but it was the best that he could do.

Carol changed the topic, and they talked about her granddaughter until light peeked in through the windows. She insisted on taking his temperature before she'd let him leave, to make sure he really didn't have hypothermia. He didn't. Before he left, she made him promise to stop by in a few days, and he found it surprisingly easy to agree.

Matt went for a walk through the neighborhood, as much to stretch his legs as to check for any new ice flows. Shady bits of sidewalk and the dips at the ends of driveways could accumulate a surprising amount of slick ice as snow melted during the day and froze overnight. He was clearing out a challenging bit under a linden tree on the next street over from his when he heard a familiar yipping.

Across the street, a teenage girl struggled to rein in a bundle of rage in the form of a Jack Russell terrier. Matt recognized it as the dog who had led him on such a chase three days ago. The dog strained at its leash, almost pulling the girl over. It seemed that the terrier remembered Matt, too. Matt no longer felt any animosity towards the poor mutt, but neither did he wish to get to know it better, so he continued on his way.

When he got home, Matt settled onto the couch, feeling tired, but not drained. He was beginning to suspect that the amulet drew power from him to work, but as long as he didn't overdo it, it didn't seem to actually hurt him. So, he was being careful. It was getting late, and he needed to start on dinner right away if he wanted to eat. He set a pot of water to boil for pasta, then started chopping the broccoli while a podcast played in the background.

Soon enough, he sat down at the dining room table to eat a home cooked meal. His plate sat in a small clearing within the chaos. It wasn't much, but it was more than he'd cleaned in months. He pushed a pile of books a little farther out of the way, and one of Olivia's character drawings fell out. He smiled at the paladin and the rogue, sleeping in a forest while a comically tiny dragon snuck up on them.

He didn't know that he believed what Carol had said, that talking about his feelings would make any sort of a difference, but he couldn't deny that he felt lighter since talking with her. And thinking back on this whole affair, it did start with the desire to help people. That was just as important as the discovery of magic—though the magic was pretty cool. Maybe he was a little bit lonely.

After he rinsed his plate and put it in the dishwasher, he grabbed his phone and texted Dave. He apologized for blowing him off for so long and asked when the group would be starting a new campaign, so he could rejoin the party. Dave immediately wrote back to let him know that he was welcome any time, that he'd write Matt's character back into the game right now, if he wanted.

Matt felt something shift and crack inside him, melting like the snow outside. He took Dave up on that offer. It would be hard, being with the gang without Olivia, but maybe it was worth doing anyway. He'd withstood a lot while using the heat amulet this past week—maybe he could survive the cracking of his frozen heart, in order to get to the human connection on the other side.

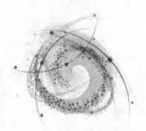

ABOUT THE AUTHOR

J.Z. Weston writes speculative short stories and reviews. They live near the Charles River with their husband and one very needy cat. You can find more of their work at: jzwestonauthor.com

HOW THE KING OF NEW ORLEANS LOST HIS HAT

BY
J LAYNE NELSON

HOW THE KING OF NEW ORLEANS LOST HIS HAT

The King of New Orleans' top hat woke up hungry. The hat had found its way to his chambers, placed itself upon his face, and began sucking out his soul. He should have gotten a cat instead. Of all his subjects, only this hat would be so impertinent. It knew his career as the city's preeminent magician had been built upon its secret.

"You're hungry, I get it," the King said.

He rose from bed like a zombie and placed the hat upon his head, its tall, black silk crown resting upon the tangled mass of his red curls. As he strolled from his bedroom, he took the hat off and pulled out a fresh, warm beignet. At least, that's what he'd thought of and expected to pull from the hat. Instead, his fingers wrapped around a cold, half-eaten, egg muffin sandwich. The willful hat defied him more often of late.

"Okay, point taken," the King muttered.

When the hat felt cooperative, the King could pull anything he wanted out of it. Well, almost anything. There were three limitations to its power: First, it could only conjure real things. Imaginary things like unicorn horns were impossible, but a narwhal tusk could be summoned. In fact, one of those hung over his fireplace mantle.

Second, the hat couldn't bring forth anything living. Ironically, if he wanted to pull a rabbit out of a hat, he would have to do it the old-fashioned way. Most important of all, the hat required offerings to work. The King discovered the hat loved bourbon, pizza, and pistachio ice cream. But above all, the hat craved money.

Nothing the hat made could be used as an offering, but he made enough money on his own to keep it satisfied, or at least he thought so.

The King picked off a spot of mold on the cold, half-eaten breakfast sandwich and took a bite and shuffled into the living room of his Royal Street apartment. He had eaten worse in the days before the hat. From his second story window he had a great view of the Hotel Monteleone and beyond into Canal Street, and soon tourists would meander their way toward dinner in the French Quarter's many bars and restaurants. The time to hold an audience drew near.

He finished breakfast and donned his royal attire. Today's ensemble made him look like a cross between Johnny Rotten and a lounge singer: ripped jeans, boots, a smart dinner jacket, white shirt, and black tie. Over this, he pulled on his signature purple trench coat lined with dozens of pockets to store props or to feed the hat in an emergency. A few coins and bills he'd received as tips the night before lay scattered on the coffee table, and he scraped them into the hat's crown. The red inner lining of the hat gave way to a black void and the money disappeared without a sound. That would hold it off for a while, but he would need more soon. He donned the hat and headed for the door.

The phone in his jeans pocket pulsed.

He pulled out the phone out and saw he had a voicemail from his father, who'd thrown him away like garbage over two years ago. The same man who'd told him his late mother would be so disappointed in him for throwing his life away to be "a homeless busker," as he recalled it. The King made it clear that he wanted to break contact, and after a few faltering attempts, the old man finally respected his wishes.

Against his better judgment, he pressed a few buttons and played the message.

"Byron, son, it's Dad. Listen, I know we haven't talked in a while, but I needed to—"

The King stopped the message short. The old man sounded tired, and perhaps a little humbled. Good for him. The King didn't have time for this. He needed to meet his subjects.

Despite the cold and dreary evening, the Quarter was still lively with tourists wrapping up their New Year's vacations. Threads of street jazz intertwined with rock, R&B, and the hum of people ready for another night of sin. The King needed to hurry if he was going to secure his prime spot near Bourbon

Street. If it was already taken, he might have to get closer to his rowdier subjects than he'd like. Drunken revelers would part with their money easily but would also scare off his audience, and the King needed an audience more than he needed a crumpled dollar bill from someone who was on their fifth hurricane.

The King drew a deck of cards from his trench coat and started working the crowd with sleight of hand tricks. Midway through dazzling a young boy with "The Four Burglars," he noticed a familiar face winding her way through the clusters of people. Instead of her usual ponytail, her hair flowed down her back like spilled ink. Her gray fleece jacket, fashionable blouse, and blue jeans heightened the beauty he had grown accustomed to seeing veiled behind her work uniform.

The King did not know her name, but in his mind, he called her the Maiden, and he had fallen in love with her by degrees. She smiled at something on her phone, and his heart ached at the sight of her as she passed out of view.

The King silently berated himself for losing focus, but he recovered as smoothly as he could, completing the trick to tepid applause. He ate his deck of cards using a bit of sleight of hand and launched into his next trick, when he spied two men following the Maiden. They moved with a studied detachment, but to someone whose livelihood depended upon reading body language, they may as well have shouted their intentions.

The King usually stayed above the fray, preferring to let the common folk resolve their disputes without his involvement, but he was no stranger to the rougher side of life in the Quarter. A veritable river of debauchery flowed through Bourbon Street, its many alleys and side streets acting like sinful tributaries. He would brook no harm coming to the Maiden. And when you have a magic hat that can conjure nearly anything, you're more than prepared when trouble comes calling.

The King cut his act short and made apologies while he plucked a fake rose from behind a man's head and gave the flower to the man's daughter. He jogged after the Maiden's two stalkers and hoped he had misjudged the situation. The hat grew warm on his head, as it did when he felt strong emotions like the anxiety creeping up his spine.

The two men continued to trail behind the Maiden but had begun to close in. One of the men, balding and large with a lumbering gait, looked over to his companion, a tall, wiry fellow with a long face, and nodded. After a moment, the Maiden turned towards Bourbon Street and crossed over to a side street. The men drew closer. They would make their move soon if the King didn't act.

"Hello gentlemen," the King said with all the regal bravery he could muster. "Could I interest you in a magic trick?"

The taller of the two men, the one who had a long face, turned to the King.

"How about one where you piss off?" he slurred.

"I insist! I won't need but a moment of your time," the King said. Beyond the two men, the Maiden moved further away.

"What's your problem, man?" the stouter of the two men said.

"None, sirs! I'm sorry to have bothered you. You both seem like you're in a hurry..." the King trailed off as the long-faced man moved to circle behind him.

"Again, my apologies, good sirs. It wasn't my intention to give offense," the King said, doffing his hat and sketching the faintest impression of a bow.

The stout man shoved the King off balance and his long-faced friend stuck out a leg to send him crashing to the wet brick of the street.

The King started to get up when Long Face swung a leg, hard, into his stomach. The King scrambled back in fear. He'd let go of the hat when he fell, but one hand closed over it, and he pulled it to him.

He looked up at the men defiantly and reached inside the hat. He expected to feel the reassuring heft of the pistol he envisioned in his mind, but instead he found nothing more than the hat's silken lining. He pulled his hand out and reached in again, this time imagining the handle of a knife, but again, the hat denied him.

"Hey Marv, you think the freak is trying pull a rabbit out of there?" Long Face said as he kicked the King again with even more force.

"Dunno, don't care," Marv said and sent a kick of his own into the King. And another.

The King groaned in pain and curled up reflexively. Despite the pain, he kept a white-knuckled grip on the hat, for all the good it had done him. The hat felt ice cold in his grip. Marv and Long Face continued kicking the King mercilessly, enjoying his cries of pain.

A feminine voice cut through the din of the King's groan and the laughter of the two drunks.

"Hey! Stop! Are you crazy? Leave him alone!" the Maiden shouted.

Marv turned to look at the woman and lurched towards her, hands out to grab her. The Maiden stepped to the side and grabbed one of Marv's outstretched arms, twisting it around his back and bending it at a sharply painful angle. The she planted one of her tennis shoes into the back of his knee and drove him down to the ground. She glared at Long Face, who was dumbstruck by how easily she controlled the now screaming Marv.

"Help! Someone call the police!" the Maiden shouted. By this point people had begun to crowd around the fight, albeit at a respectable distance. The King finally managed to roll from his side onto his knees.

Long Face took stock of the situation and half stumbled, half ran back towards Bourbon Street. The Maiden released Marv and he rose to follow suit, limping after his friend.

"Need help getting up?" The Maiden moved to the King and offered a hand.

"N-no I-I don't," the King said.

Shaking, he attempted to get to his feet, and nearly stumbled but the Maiden took his arm and helped him rise.

"They were kicking you pretty hard. You sure you're okay? You don't want to go to the police? Or maybe the ER?"

The King, still a bit dazed, shook his head vigorously, and gingerly placed the top hat back on his head, which still felt unnaturally cold. The last thing he wanted to do was speak to the police and run the risk of anyone discovering his hat's powers, even if the hat had refused to help him when he needed it. He still didn't understand why. Didn't he feed it enough? The hat could be temperamental, but he couldn't believe it would let him be seriously hurt or wouldn't help him in a potentially life and death situation.

But it had done just that.

"Are you sure you're okay? You kinda spaced out there," The Maiden said.

"Apologies, milady," the King said.

"Milady? Can't say I've been called that before. I'm Monica," she said, stepping away from him.

"I'm the King," the King said.

"Really? You don't look like an Elvis impersonator."

A weak smile lit the King's face and heat rose in his cheeks.

"Do you want to go somewhere to settle your nerves at least? I know a little cafe not too far from here. Come on. I'll buy you a drink," Monica said and started walking back down the street.

The King, still reeling, followed.

Monica guided the King to a small, cramped cafe typical of the many dives in the French Quarter. The main room would have been better described as a glorified hallway, just wide enough for a well-stocked bar, several stools, and a couple of small tables. Beyond the main room was another, slightly larger room where a small bar and a food service window ran along one wall. Monica motioned for the King to take a seat at one of the high-top tables across from the bar.

He sat, still bewildered that Monica, who he imagined meeting so many times, had saved him from being beaten and now would be buying him a drink.

From behind the service window, an elderly man with streaks of black in his otherwise silver hair peered out in surprise.

"Monica, I thought you were off today? Tell me ya not here about your paycheck, because I checked and made sure the direct deposit went through this time," the man said. His words were flavored with more than a little Cajun accent.

"No, no, Johnny. I'm not here about my paycheck, but thank you. I thought this guy could use a drink," she said, pointing to where the King sat.

Johnny blinked and looked at him for a moment, then recognition blossomed across his face with a grin.

"Hey that's the King of New Orleans you got there!" he said. "How'd you get him here?"

"What?" Monica said.

"Ya know, the King of New Orleans. He's like…a magician. Does magic tricks for the kids and tourists. Ain't that right, your majesty?" Johnny made a caricature of a bow, but the man's words held warmth. The King had found a loyal subject.

The King straightened himself and regained an echo of his royal composure.

"Yes, I am the King of New Orleans," he said.

"Does 'the King' actually have a name?" Monica asked, a bemused smirk curling one side of her mouth.

"I'm just the King," he said.

"Okay, Mr. Just The King. You've got a drink on me. What'll you have?" she said.

"Just coffee, thank you."

Alcohol presented too much risk that he'd do something stupid with the hat, or worse, say something stupid in front of Monica. A small price to pay for getting almost anything else you wanted. Assuming he still could.

"We'll take a coffee and a Sazerac, Johnny, if you could," Monica said.

"It's not like you don't know where it where it is," Johnny chuckled.

"I'm not the one working right now, Johnny, you are!" Monica said in mostly feigned exasperation.

"I'll be right back," she said as she went to make their drinks.

The King reached into the hat again and thought of oxycodone. Nothing happened. He then thought of Tylenol, then something simpler like a can of soup, and finally a scrap of paper. Still, the hat refused to respond. Perhaps its magic ran out? No, the King could still feel the hat reacting to him. It no longer felt cold, but as he held it, he could feel…discomfort. The hat was not pleased. As Monica returned, he set the hat back on the table.

"You take cream and sugar? All we've got is the powdered stuff," she said as she placed packets of cream and sugar on the table.

The King took three packs of sugar and poured them into the steaming mug.

"Black as night and sweet as sin. That's how my abuela drinks it. It doesn't taste like coffee anymore with that much sugar in it, at least not to me," she said, sipping her Sazerac.

The King sipped his coffee, trying to look regal while struggling to think of something clever to say. His tongue felt heavy as lead.

"So, how'd you get mixed up with those guys?" Monica said.

The King felt heat rise up his neck to his cheeks. "I guess they just didn't appreciate me trying to show them some magic. No more guerrilla street magic for me," he said.

He would not admit how wanted to protect her. Especially after how spectacularly poor his attempted rescue turned out.

"Is it always so dangerous being a magician around here?" she asked.

"Usually, no. Unless you have to deal with drunk people. Most of the time, my subjects are happy to see me work." He crossed his right hand over his left, produced a fake yellow rose and offered it to her.

"Oh, and there's the magic. Thanks." Monica smiled, and the sweetness of it made butterflies dance in his stomach.

"Why did you want to be a magician?" she asked and took another sip of her drink.

"I thought magic was cool. Growing up I wanted to be a real wizard but settled for learning conventional magic. I wanted to become famous like Houdini or Copperfield. My parents, especially my dad, thought I was wasting my life and… Well, now I'm a professional magician," he said. How long had it been since he had opened up to someone?

"Oh, I'm sorry. I didn't realize," Monica said. "I didn't mean to bring up a bad memory. I can't imagine what that must be like. I lost both of my parents early—car accident. Abuela raised me, and we're so close. I just can't imagine not having that kind of support in my life. That must have been hard on you," she said with genuine concern.

The memory of his dad taking him to his first magic show came back to him then. They had been close once, especially after his mom died. But that was over.

"It's okay. I'm doing what I love, and that's something."

"So, why call yourself the King of New Orleans? It doesn't sound very...magical?"

"You ask a lot of questions," the King said, looking into his coffee. "New Orleans has a Mayor, but no King, so I decided to fill the vacancy."

He left out the part where he'd walked out on his father after an argument and didn't look back. New Orleans was close enough to get to with almost no money and, luckily for him, it offered the perfect venue to hone his craft.

"Monica, where did you learn to take down big guys like that?"

Johnny barked out a laugh from the kitchen. "Watch out, King! She's a killer!"

Monica rolled her eyes. "Well, I tend bar here, but I also teach mixed martial arts and jiu jitsu. I've always believed in taking care of myself, especially where the drunks make stupid decisions and think I'm here to be groped. I'm lucky to be able to protect myself."

"I'm not sure what would have happened without you. Thanks. I hope I didn't mess up your plans too badly. You look nice."

He tried to keep his face from flushing, which only made it worse.

"I was heading to a date, but it's just a dating app kind of thing. I should let him know we need to reschedule," Monica said as she pulled out her phone. "Besides, you needed help, and I couldn't stand there and do nothing."

The King felt himself deflate inside just a little. Part of him felt guilty for ruining her date, part of him felt relieved, which in turn made him feel more guilty.

"Plenty of other people did," he said. Loyal subjects, indeed.

"Well, I'm not other people," Monica said, setting her phone on the table.

"If you need to go, I can manage."

"It's okay, he'll understand. Or he won't, and then I'll know not to waste my time. It's not every day I get to meet a King."

"I..." The King trailed off and glanced at the hat.

Monica waited, her eyebrows slightly raised.

The King said nothing for a moment, studying her face. There was something in her eyes, an earnestness, that the King used to have. When did he lose that?

He took a breath and began.

"I got a call from my dad today. First one in a while. We...aren't on speaking terms. Not sure if I want to call him back."

Monica looked a little surprised.

"Sorry, you've done so much already, and here I am making you a therapist," he said.

"No, it's alright. I did say I'm a bartender. Do you want to patch things up?"

"I don't know if talking to him would actually solve anything."

"Are you happy with your life right now? Without him in it?"

The King glanced over at the hat again. It fell off the table, landing on its crown.

"Guess the ghosts are here already," Monica said.

If only she knew, the King thought.

"Right now, I have pretty much anything I want. I'm successful in my career. I have a great apartment I barely stay in and a nice car I almost never drive. I thought it would be enough, but it feels so empty," he said.

"It's nice to have nice things, and I'm sure you worked hard for them. But if you don't have people in your life you can share them with, what does it matter?"

The King barely worked at all. The hat gave him all the money he wanted. He hadn't earned anything.

"I don't know how to change. And I don't know if talking to Dad will actually solve anything," he said.

Monica reached out to touch the King's arm.

"Everybody changes. But the changes that matter? You take a chance on those. Don't wake up and wish you had called him back when you had the chance. If I could talk to my parents again, there's almost nothing I wouldn't do," she said.

"You've given me something to think about," the King said.

"Take a leap of faith, whatever you decide," she said, patting his arm.

They sat in silence for a while and finished their drinks. Monica called a rideshare to take the King back to his apartment.

As the car arrived, she called out to him.

"Hey, King. Nice meeting you. I'll come check out a show sometime," she said, waving.

"My name, it's Byron. Just, keep it a secret, okay?"

Monica curtseyed. "Of course, your majesty."

"Thank you, milady," he said, dipping into the best bow his bruised ribs could handle before gingerly stepping into the car for the short ride home. The King trudged up the stairs to his apartment, walked straight back to his bed, and fell into a fitful sleep.

The King's eyes popped open in alarm. He couldn't breathe. The hat had sealed itself over his face. The King was about to be murdered by his own crown.

He fell out of his bed and crashed to the floor, straining against the hat, which had fastened itself to him like a giant suction cup. Frantic and seeing spots, he fumbled around in his coat pockets until he found a small knife that he wished he'd remembered the day before.

He opened the knife by touch and tried stabbing the hat. Strangely, the velvet crown of the hat deflected the blade as if it were tough leather.

As a last resort, he tried jamming the knife between his face and the bottom of the hat. He worked the point left and right, feeling a hot sting of pain as blood began to stream down his face.

Eventually, he found purchase under the hat and pulled. The hat came free at last, and he felt a small stream of air fill his lungs. With his vigor renewed, he pulled again and this time the hat came free.

Months ago, on a muggy June night, he took the hat off a guy sleeping on a bench in Louis Armstrong Park. The hat was sitting on that man's face just like it had been on his own. The hat killed its previous owner the same way it just tried to kill him.

The King looked down at his fabulous, poisonous top hat. He then looked around at his well-appointed living room inside his fashionable loft apartment and realized he had nothing that mattered. A car he never drove, clothes he never wore, all of it meaningless. The hat gave him all these things as it stole his independence, his courage, and his faith in his own magic.

It turned out that the King of New Orleans really could have almost anything he wanted, all it would cost was his soul.

Was a king still a king without his crown?

Time to find out.

The King put his hand on the crown of the top hat and pushed. He expected to crumple it with ease, but it resisted. The King pushed again, harder this time, until he was straining, wiry cords of muscle rippling in his forearms. He tried standing on it, jumping on it, nothing worked.

He went to his bed, pulled out a duffel bag and unzipped it. Money he'd taken from the hat over time filled the bag to bursting. It wouldn't be able to regain power from things it produced, but he wanted nothing the hat could offer. Not anymore. Never again.

He took out a few straps of twenties and dropped them into the hat one by one. Each of them fell as if into a void with no bottom. He scooped out more money, some twenties, some fifties and even hundreds this time, and dumped them into the hat. Piles of bills were swallowed almost immediately. He took the duffel bag and shook it, causing more cash to pour out of it and into the hat. The hat seemed unfazed.

He looked at his smartwatch. He'd taken it from the hat. He took it off and dropped it in. He walked through his apartment and found things he either took from the hat or paid for using hat money. With a regretful sigh, he dropped the narwhal horn in last. Finally, the hat undulated. The King pushed on the hat's crown again.

Slowly, by degrees, it began to give. As the King strained to crumple the hat, the cursed thing abandoned all pretense and pushed into his psyche. The malevolent will of the hat, fully exposed in his mind's eye, assaulted him with flashes of images.

Memories of previous owners stretching back over centuries tore through his mind, back to a time when plantations lined the crescent of Lake Pontchartrain. All these memories culminated with the death of any foolish enough to believe they had mastered the hat.

The King felt his mind being peeled like an onion.

He struggled desperately to hold on to who he was. Memories of his own slipped by and he struggled to hold on to them. Memories of the first magic show he saw with his dad, learning magic on his own and showing his parents. His mom and dad clapping excitedly after he successfully completed his first card trick. Becoming a performing magician who delighted his subjects. Slowly, the King's own memories came back to the forefront of his mind. He anchored himself in those happy moments and found himself again.

He was the King of New Orleans, and he earned that himself. He didn't need a crown.

The texture of the hat began to feel rougher, less like silk and more like leather. The lights in the apartment began to flicker, he kept pushing.

Soon bulbs burst in their sockets, there was a screeching, nails-on-chalkboard noise as the crown began to tear.

The King kept pushing.

The hat began to feel warm; its psychic assault grew shrill and desperate.

The King kept pushing.

The King fell back against his living room wall, pushed with all his strength, screaming as he did. The crown tore away with an inhuman wail, and his hand burst through the other side. What remained of the hat crumbled into dust. He slid to the ground feeling exhausted and held his jacket to his bleeding face. He sat there, leaning against the wall, until the sun shifted across the sky and gave way to twilight.

He felt fatigued, like a part of him was missing, but also a sense of relief, like a dislocated joint had just been set back into place after a long period of chronic pain.

The King rose on shaky legs and walked to his dresser, pulled his phone from a drawer, hit a few buttons, and raised it to his ear.

Time to take a leap of faith.

"Hello?" a voice crackled to life on the other end. "Byron…is that you?"

"Hi, Dad. Yeah, it's me."

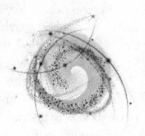

ABOUT THE AUTHOR

J Layne Nelson was born in a city of iron and magic better known as Birmingham, Alabama. When he's not rolling d20s or exploring new places, he writes horror and fantasy in many flavors. He currently lives in Miami, Florida.

THE MIRROR
BY
ANNIE PERCIK

THE MIRROR

Jane leaned back precariously from her perch atop a wooden stool, checking whether or not the mirror was straight. The mirror was large, with an ornate gilded frame; not the sort of thing she would normally buy. It had been quite a task to affix it to the wall on her own. She was distracted for a moment by the reflection of Timmy, her son, who was sitting on the floor behind her, playing with some blocks. He had managed to create a wobbly tower of three and was surveying his achievement with obvious pleasure. He reached out with both chubby hands, as if planning to hug the blocks to him, and it was no surprise to Jane when he knocked them to the floor. He let out a wail of despair and turned a bawling face in her direction, seeking comfort.

Jane climbed down from the stool, crossed the carpet, and scooped him into her arms.

"Now, then," she said, stroking his hair. "There's no need for that. They're only blocks. Shall we see how high we can build them if we work together?"

She sat down on the floor with Timmy in front of her, and was soon absorbed in the play, the mirror forgotten.

It had been an impulsive purchase. Jane and Timmy had been taking their usual Thursday walk through the park when Jane spotted a market that had been set up nearby. She left their normal route to take a look, weaving Timmy's pushchair through the other people perusing the stalls. There was a range of different wares on offer: cakes and biscuits, jewellery and ornaments, greetings cards and notebooks. Jane worked out a path that took in every stall, pointing out colourful items to Timmy and stopping every now and then to examine something more closely. She wasn't tempted to buy anything, though, until she reached the very last stall, which had a staggering array of mirrors of all sizes, shapes, and styles. Jane stopped, overwhelmed by the multitude of reflections looking back at her. She wished she had taken a bit more time over her appearance that morning. The combination of messy hair and rumpled clothing didn't give the best impression, though at least Timmy was clean and neatly turned out. She reached up to smooth her hair behind her ears, wondering if she had an elastic band in her bag to tie it back.

"See one that takes your fancy?" a voice said, pulling Jane's attention to the woman behind the counter.

She was old, her face a mass of wrinkles. Her dark eyes peered out from beneath a colourful headscarf which hid her hair entirely. She was dressed in an assortment of brightly patterned layers; they reflected back out of the mirrors behind her, making the stall look festive. She smiled encouragingly at Jane.

"Oh, no," Jane said, embarrassed at being caught examining herself, and not wanting the woman to be mistaken about her intention to buy something. "I really can't afford..."

She trailed off as one of the mirrors caught her eye. It was off to one side, propped up against the stall, separate from the others. Jane wheeled Timmy's pushchair right up to it. He waved at himself and giggled happily as his reflection waved back. Jane reached out and traced the carved pattern of the gilt frame with her fingers. The mirror was much too large for her front room, and the frame would look garish amongst her drab, utilitarian furniture. But it was a striking piece, imposing and with a baroque grandeur that appealed to her. It reminded her of the seventeenth century manor house where Timmy's father, Dan, had proposed over high tea; a bittersweet memory since his death the year before, but one that prompted a strong desire to own the mirror. Jane had no idea how she would get it home, though. It was too big for her to carry it by herself even if she hadn't had Timmy with her.

"I could get my nephew to deliver it tomorrow afternoon, if you like," the stallholder said, as if Jane had spoken aloud.

"That would be lovely," Jane heard herself say as she pulled her purse out of her pocket.

The transaction was the work of a moment, and Jane provided her address for the delivery. Then she and Timmy went on their way, their usual routine re-establishing itself as soon as they were out of the market. When the stallholder's burly nephew delivered the mirror the next day, Jane discovered the wall over the fireplace was exactly the right place for it. In fact, it made the room appear much larger once it was secured.

Jane didn't give the mirror much thought over the next few days, until she came to dust the mantelpiece about a week after buying it. She was manoeuvring her feather duster between the ornaments in a desultory fashion, thinking about Dan. It was just over a year since his death, and the loss of him still crept up on her unexpectedly.

She caught sight of Timmy's reflection behind her in the mirror. But she had dropped Timmy off at nursery hours ago. She spun round in alarm: no Timmy. She turned slowly back to the mirror; there he was again, sitting on the floor with his blocks. As she watched, he reached out and knocked over the tower he had made. His face scrunched up in despair, but there was no accompanying noise. Jane was even more shocked when a separate reflection of herself came into view and comforted Timmy before sitting down with him on the floor to play with the blocks.

The memory came back; that had happened the day she had hung the mirror up on the wall, nearly a week before. How could the mirror be showing her a scene that had occurred in the past? Seconds later, the phantom Jane and Timmy faded away, leaving the reflections of the room, and Jane herself, as they should be. Jane wasn't sure what she should do. She wanted to tell someone, but who would believe her? She had no evidence of what had just happened, and anyone she spoke to about it would think she was mad. Maybe she was.

Over the next few days, Jane watched the mirror carefully. The phenomenon repeated nearly every day, but frustratingly only when she was alone. She invited her sister round for tea one afternoon to try and catch it out, but the mirror remained stubbornly rooted in reality the entire time. As soon as her sister left, though, it showed Jane several snippets of activity that had taken place within its reflective sphere during the previous week.

The following Thursday, Jane took Timmy to the park as usual, and looked eagerly for the market, hoping to be able to ask the stallholder about the mirror. But the market wasn't there.

Eventually, Jane just got used to the mirror's odd quirks, and found it quite comforting to have Timmy's reflection available to her when he wasn't actually in the flat. The scenes were never from longer than a week ago, and only ever lasted a few minutes at most, but it became an interesting game to predict when it might happen and what it might show. It made Jane feel as if she had access to a precious resource of visual memories, a lovely accompaniment to her daily routine.

Of course, the scenes the mirror chose to show weren't always those of an idyllic domestic life. Jane was human, after all, and taking care of Timmy on her own had its challenges. On one occasion, the mirror showed her in stained pyjamas, hair so unkempt a scarecrow would be ashamed of it, wandering blearily around the front room in a pre-coffee daze. Was the mirror passing judgement on her? Jane became very self-conscious for a while after that, taking care that the mirror could only capture her in her best light.

On a morning some weeks after the mirror had first revealed its power, Jane had just made herself a steaming mug of green tea and carried it through to the front room. It was the first chance she'd had to sit down all morning, and she was very much looking forward to a few moments of relaxation. Timmy had had a bad night teething, and Jane had spent much of it trying to soothe his shrill crying. He seemed much better now and was happily playing on the floor with one of his trains, but Jane could not recover so quickly and was suffering with a throbbing head. She put the cup of tea down on the coffee table and was about to collapse into the sofa cushions when the doorbell rang.

"Oh, what now?" she cried, stomping out of the room and flinging the front door open.

A woman stood on the doorstep, her smile as bright as her lipstick.

"We're canvassing the neighbourhood," she said, waving a clipboard in Jane's face. "Would you sign our petition...?"

Jane didn't give her a chance to finish her sentence, cutting her off with an abrupt, "Not interested."

She almost slammed the door in the woman's face and stalked back to the front room. She was about to finally sit down on the sofa, when she spotted that the picture of Dan on the mantelpiece was askew. In her frustrated mood, this prompted a surge of annoyance, so she crossed the room in two quick steps and reached up to straighten it. She caught sight of some movement in the mirror and focused on Timmy. As she watched, transfixed, he pulled himself up to a standing position—the first time he had ever done such a thing—holding onto the edge of the coffee table to steady himself. Jane found herself completely unable to move or react as Timmy stretched one hand out towards her mug of boiling tea and tipped it all over himself. In the mirror, his reflection screamed in shock and pain, but she couldn't hear him.

As if released from some kind of spell, Jane could move again. If this accident had already happened, how could she have not noticed Timmy crying when she came back into the room? Heart in her throat, she turned to see Timmy still sitting calmly on the floor, pushing his train along the carpet. It rolled slightly under the coffee table, and he scooted forwards to follow it. When he encountered the edge of the table, he regarded it solemnly for a long moment, then grabbed hold of it and pulled himself to his feet. Jane rushed over and picked up her mug of tea before he could reach for it. She deposited it on the top of a nearby bookcase, then collapsed onto the sofa, looking from her son to the mirror and back again.

Timmy gazed at her with an exquisitely smug expression on his face, clearly waiting for some kind of response. Jane's mind was numb with horror at how stupid she had been to leave her tea unattended, but Timmy was obviously unaware of the danger he had been in and would probably be upset by a dramatic overreaction.

"Darling! What a clever boy!" Jane cried, forcing herself to focus on his achievement, rather than the narrowly avoided tragedy. Timmy's face split into a triumphant grin.

Jane reached out and hugged Timmy to her, relief at his miraculous escape warring with amazement at the mirror's new ability to look into the future. She glanced back up at their reflection and caught her breath sharply. For the briefest of instants, she thought she saw the image of Dan standing behind the sofa, his arms spread protectively behind them. Jane blinked through sudden tears and he was gone. Surely a trick of her imagination, brought on by the emotion of the moment. She hugged Timmy more tightly and wondered.

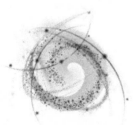

ABOUT THE AUTHOR

Annie Percik lives in London, writing novels and short stories, whilst working as a freelance editor (https://alobear.co.uk/?page_id=778). She writes a blog about writing on her website (https://alobear.co.uk/), which is where all her current publications are listed, including her novels, The Defiant Spark (http://getbook.at/DefiantSpark) and A Spectrum of Heroes (https://markosia.com/a-spectrum-of-heroes/). She hosts a media review podcast (https://stillloveit.libsyn.com/), and publishes a photo-story blog, recording the adventures of her teddy bear (https://aloysius-bear.dreamwidth.org/). He is much more popular online than she is.

SOME KIND OF MAGIC

BY
JACKIE ROSS FLAUM

SOME KIND OF MAGIC

The woman filled the doorway to Socrates Gray's apartment with her bulk, sturdy walking stick, and oversized personality.

"My grandson need your help." Tituba Mitchell thudded her stick across the wood threshold. Pinned by her dark eyes, Gray understood why she was a force in the 1970 Black community of Hartford, Connecticut.

He'd lived next door for six months and she'd only nodded to him. Now her red and orange earrings swayed as Tituba walked into his apartment like they were old friends. She plopped in a well-worn club chair before an open window then reached across a side table to turn the oscillating fan until her silver-streaked hair blew behind her.

Gray took refuge on the sofa across from her. He was a tall, well-built man with an Afro that needed trimming, but Tituba made him feel small, almost like a boy. The full moon drowned out the city lights to shine through the window on his guest.

"What can I do for you, Tituba?" he asked.

"My grandson need somethin' investigated."

Gray smiled. "I'm an office worker on Main—"

Tituba rolled her eyes, and her head lolled to one side. "Sterling Brothers Limited, detectives. You and a white woman name a Madeline Sterling. You 'the brothers.'"

She'd done her homework. He only hoped she hadn't dug too deeply. He and Tituba lived in the poorest section of Hartford, where gossip and storytelling were coins of the realm, prized forms of entertainment. If she'd heard stories about him, he'd heard stranger ones about her. The foul smells from her apartment supported claims that Tituba cooked potions handed down from her ancestor and namesake, the Black witch of the Salem trials.

One side of Tituba's mouth curled in a half-smile. Gray felt like a prey with Tituba ready to pounce.

"What's the problem? Sterling and I are happy to help." His promise to involve Sterling came easily. They had been partners for six years, most of it investigating the murders of civil rights workers in the South.

"My grandson Jonah's the first in the family to go to college. This his freshman year," Tituba said with a proud lift of her chins.

"Jonah seems like a fine fellow," Gray said. "May I offer you a soda?"

"He won Civic Scholarship Project scholarship." Tituba waved aside his offer. "Now the woman running the Project got him workin' like a bank mule."

"Is community service part of the scholarship?" Gray asked.

"Na." Sweat rolled off Tituba. She rearranged her orange and red caftan while she appeared to do the same for her thoughts. "But he got to do what the Project director say or she'll get the board to call off his money."

"Is she asking Jonah to do something illegal?" Gray asked.

"Huh! People knows what'd I'd do to anybody try that."

The gossips at the bar next door said Tituba cast spells that paralyzed people. That's how she could beat a local drug dealer with her cane for tempting Jonah. Her grandson must have been in elementary school and Tituba lighter on her feet then. The bar crowd also claimed she cut off a gang leader's manhood for pressuring her cousin to join. Gray had no explanation for that one. Whatever power Tituba had in her youth made her fearsome into old age. Even Hartford cops stepped aside for her.

If only half the tales about her were true, Jonah's problem sounded like one Tituba should be able to manage alone.

"Have you talked to the Project board members?" Gray said.

"They afraid of her! They don't want no protests or marches at their businesses or-r the neighborhood people getting up in their faces. 'Specially them white board members. They skeered the most!"

Gray's mind flashed on his petite partner, who wasn't scared of anything, even things that should frighten a sane person.

"Board members say they can only give money to kids on Alice Tower's list—that the sister runnin' the Project," Tituba continued. "She takes all the records and locks 'em up. The board can't get names of students or see financial records. If they ask, Alice jest get pissy. She and her brother ain't nobody to mess with.

Her brother, Nathan Burundi, pastors the Missionary Apostolic Church of the Deliverance near Weaver High."

Burundi. Now he got it. Gray's friends in the civil rights movement had mentioned him. Pastor Burundi had returned from desegregation marches to take his father's pulpit. Since his arrival, every North End protest began at Burundi's church, physically or spiritually.

"What's Mrs. Tower asking Jonah to do?"

"She got him babysitting her kids, washing her clothes, getting her groceries, sweepin' her house. That boy don't have time for nuthing. He got to earn spending money for school." Tituba shifted, causing the chair to creak in an ominous manner. "He ain't the only child she workin' neither."

Gray's eyebrow arched.

"It seem mighty strange everybody who get a scholarship go to Missionary church. They don't when they win, but they go there when they come home. They gotta tithe and do 'volunteer' work too," Tituba continued.

"How many students are we talking about?" Gray said.

"A lot."

Not helpful. Gray tried something else.

"Are the students working for the church or Alice Tower?"

Tituba shrugged. "Not all students come home for summer. There's thirty or forty of 'em here. She got most students jobs tutoring kids in programs around the city, and some go to towns nearby. Then, they fills out mileage reports and has to give her part of that money."

"The parents are okay with this?" Gray asked.

Tituba harrumphed. "Two years ago, Jacintha Williams and her mama makes a big fuss about the work and kickbacks. Jacintha lost her scholarship. Now she waitressin' at a diner down on the Silas Deane. Her mama lost her job at Colt after Pastor Burundi say she steal church money. He forgived her so she didn't go to jail."

Pastor Burundi and his sister apparently had a lot of power and no scruples about using it. Gray's jaw tightened.

"People more skeerd of them than me," Tituba admitted.

Gray couldn't imagine it.

"Now, Alice have people do anything for her. True believers—kids she helped from the start. Alice done SOME good." Tituba rocked back in the seat and made one, two, three attempts to rise before she succeeded. Once on her feet, the moonlight streaming through the open window struck her back until she glowed.

Gray's mouth dropped.

"Ain't you never seen magic come down?" Tituba guffawed and hobbled to the door. Gray followed, slightly awed.

As she turned to walk out, two damp manila folders suddenly appeared in her hand. She slapped them against his chest.

"My sister work at the school board, and Jonah need his scholarship. Be quick—and be quiet," Tituba said.

Gray didn't want to think where those folders had been hiding.

Madeline Sterling barely concealed her excitement at welcoming her first and only appointment, Bethany Abernathy of Avon, Junior League president. Sterling had eaten a lot of rubber chicken dinners and attended dozens of Chamber of Commerce meetings to attract a client like her. A paying client.

The two women sat in the conference area Sterling had created in the Hartford office. She had furnished it with a chair, a coffee table, a loveseat, and two potted plants. The plants, despite shameful neglect, reached from the floor to the middle of the windows. They provided a distraction from the second-hand furniture and faded green walls.

The office on Main Street near the Old State House was in a respectable building, and the rent wasn't bad—important factors when Sterling and Gray picked Hartford to start their detective agency. A bonus: she was close to her parents in Boston and thousands of miles from Gray's trouble in the South.

While they waited for her partner, Sterling got basic information from her client such as billing address. The woman, who folded her hands in her lap, appeared to be about Sterling's age, early twenties. Miss Abernathy's teased brown hair parted on the side and her dress hugged her body. Sterling brushed aside one of her unruly curls and wished she had worn another suit. She chose it to set off her blue eyes, an unusual color for red-haired people, but the skirt hung loosely on her slim body.

After Gray arrived, Miss Abernathy got to the point. "The Junior League wants to fund several worthy inner-city projects— education programs that help underprivileged youth. But we, ah, we don't know if we've chosen wisely."

"Isn't this something you could learn by visiting and talking to people in the programs?" Gray asked.

Miss Abernathy twisted her diamond engagement ring. "We tried. We were well received at their offices and work sites. But we're not comfortable with what we learned."

"Did you pick recipients?" Sterling asked.

Miss Abernathy handed Sterling a folder. "My board approved these. The funds will be allocated in September."

Sterling gaped at the figures beside each organization on the list. No wonder the Junior League was well received.

"Are any of your members on the boards of these groups?" Gray asked.

Miss Abernathy shook her head. "We wanted programs serving educational needs, and we do have members with connections to the city schools—a teacher at Bulkeley High, a counselor at Weaver High, and so forth. My brother-in-law also serves on the Hartford Board of Education."

Sterling handed the folder to Gray.

"I don't want to be hoodwinked," Miss Abernathy said. "It would reflect badly on us."

Gray showed the list of lucky organizations to Miss Abernathy. "Is there one that worries you more than the others?"

Miss Abernathy hesitated. "These two."

Sterling could read her partner well, could almost feel the zing racing through him.

"We'll get back to you with something as soon as we can," Sterling promised Miss Abernathy.

After the door closed behind their client, Sterling turned to Gray. "There's more to this, isn't there?"

Gray told her of his moonlight visitor and shared what Tituba had given him on the Civic Scholarship.

"Why doesn't she just cast a spell on them?" Sterling chuckled.

"I asked her that this morning."

Sterling's jaw dropped. Socrates Gray was the smartest man and greatest detective she'd ever known. He sounded ridiculous.

"She said the moonlight magic didn't work like that," he went on. "It wasn't like the magic of the sun or the stars. The moonlight was for trickery and deceit. And she also didn't know how potent it would be since it hit her through a window."

"Stop. Just stop." Sterling waved both hands in front of her. "I can't believe you're talking about moonlight magic the way we talk about real clues."

"'There are more things beneath heaven and earth than you know, Sterling, than are dreamt of in your philosophy.'"

"Thank you, Hamlet." Sterling sighed.

"I'm not saying I take her magic seriously," Gray said, "but I won't dismiss it either."

"We should take Alice Tower and her brother seriously. They sound vicious. It's been a long time since we handled vicious." Sterling paused. "You ready?"

Her steady gaze was meant to remind him of the murder charge he would face if anyone discovered who he was. He had killed in self-defense, but Southern law enforcement sometimes glossed over such details when their own died.

"This landed on my doorstep," he said. "I'll stay away from the cops and let you deal with them, as we decided. I can't say I'm not apprehensive, but if I backed off——."

"Tituba would hex you."

Gray smirked. "I'll take the Civic Scholarship Project."

"I'll look into the Community Scholarship Program." Sterling said to his back.

Sterling's first 'ah-ha' moment came during her call to the library's information line. The smooth, deep male voice from the library told her Community Scholarship, a program of the Hartford school board, was run by Mrs. Alice Tower. She also served as director of the non-profit Civic Project.

"The names of the program are hard to tell apart," Sterling remarked.

"It is confusing," the librarian admitted. "We've misfiled several *Hartford Courant* newspaper clippings on these two groups. Here's another from *The Hartford Times* about the Project group objecting to the school superintendent and, oh, the most recent clipping says they're also calling for the superintendent's removal."

"Why?"

The librarian read a *Courant* story saying the superintendent had ordered an audit of the board's Community Program. The Project supporters saw it as an attack on scholarship help for minority students.

No wonder Miss Abernathy wanted an outsider to investigate the two scholarship groups. Her brother-in-law and league members needed protection from the wrath of strong political figures as much as Tituba did.

Sterling hurried out of the office, rode the creaky elevator to the ground floor, and opened the front door. The day was hot. Exhaust pipe fumes from passing vehicles mingled with humidity and garbage that awaited pickup. Still, it was good to be out of the office.

She walked the dozen blocks to the school board office on High Street, saluting the old State House as she passed. The original Connecticut capitol building squatted proud and defiant amid modern high-rises, cars, and G. Fox or Sage Allen shoppers. Such endurance cheered Sterling.

Several blocks later, Sterling arrived at the Hartford school board administration office, housed in a Victorian-era building. She climbed the three wide cement steps, opened one of the building's two outer doors, and let the air-conditioning welcome her. A directory posted on a wall inside lead her to Alice Tower's Community Relations office.

No one was sitting at Community Relations' front desk, but behind it an attractive Black woman in a red mini-dress stared at papers on a desk. She looked like a professional model with her hair smoothed into a tight bun in the back that made her high cheeks and narrow face more pronounced.

"Excuse me, I'm looking for Alice Tower? The Community Scholarship director?"

The woman gave Sterling a once-over. "I'm Mrs. Tower. Can I help you?"

"I don't want to bother you, especially without an appointment," Sterling gushed. "I can see you have tons of work. I'm Madeline Sterling, and I'm doing a pamphlet for the Junior League on opportunities for young people."

At the words 'Junior League,' Alice brightened.

"Please, come in. I'll be happy to talk with you. Let me move my secretary's chair so you can sit."

"Are you sure? I hate to take up your time if you're busy." Even as she spoke, Sterling sat in the chair and pulled a notebook from her purse.

"What would you like to know?" Alice asked.

Sterling asked a few bland questions about who picked scholarship winners, how long board's Scholarship Program had existed, and its budget. Alice gave her answers and a budget sheet.

"Do the school guidance counselors who guide students to the board's Scholarship Program also select the winners?" Sterling asked.

"The school board has specific criteria for winners." Alice reached into a desk drawer and drew out a piece of paper. "The sixty winners receive $600 a semester. That's also on the sheet I gave you."

"Do you have a list of their names and where they go to college?" Sterling asked.

Alice had already reached into her file drawer again. "I'm sure I can find a list of previous winners too. Ah, here. Several students have graduated and gone to work for Connecticut Insurance."

"You said the scholarship covered tuition, but how do students afford the room and board?" Sterling noticed the moment Alice's guard went up.

"Most have summer jobs or work at their colleges," Alice's tone became brisker.

"How do you help your scholarship winners stay in school?" Sterling maintained an innocent air.

"We only provide the scholarship money—and I help with the high school counseling program at the board office. We don't work with the students once they graduate from high school."

Sterling's face fell. "Oh, I thought counseling, college visits, and tutoring help were part of your program."

"The non-profit Civic Project gives scholarships, counseling, college visits, and tutoring help." Alice leaned back in her chair. "I am the Project director, but I mostly provide technical advice to the board. They're separate groups that help minority students."

"How convenient," Sterling cried. She began with some general questions, which Alice answered in as few words as possible.

Then Sterling asked, "What's the Project budget?"

"It's public record that we raised $44,000 last year from businesses and the community."

"Impressive. May I have a list of current Project winners? And an operating budget?" Sterling leaned forward.

"That's private." Alice rose. "I'm a school board employee from nine to five. I have to get back to that job."

"Sorry to have taken so much time." Sterling held out her hand, and Alice shook it. The woman's hand felt cold and clammy. "When could we talk about the Project?"

"I can't say. I'm swamped with work." Alice folded her arms across her chest.

Thus dismissed, Sterling wandered back into the wide central hallway. Before she turned for the exit, she stopped in a few open offices to talk. At the superintendent's office she found his secretary was very chatty. The secretary spoke in glowing terms about the board's good work through the Civic Project, apparently unaware the board had nothing to do with it.

Sterling emerged from the board office more confused than before. She invented a chant to keep the two groups separate in her mind: board funds Program, private funds Project. She planned on talking to students on the Program's list.

"Board funds Program, private funds Project," she chanted over and over as she started walking back to her office.

Suddenly she wasn't alone on High Street. A battered old Ford with several young Black teenagers let out a passenger behind her. From the fleeting glance Sterling had of him, her college-age follower was taller than her and built like a football player.

Whatever his other skills, he couldn't tail someone inconspicuously.

Once she got to Main Street, Sterling crossed the street. Her follower did too. She stopped to admire something in the G. Fox store display, and he stared at something in an adjacent window. He shifted his feet and thrust both hands in his jeans pockets as he tried to make his glances at her appear nonchalant.

It wouldn't do for him to discover she was a detective, and it was too hot to walk around the city until she lost him. She went into the store, trailed by her shadow.

Walking rapidly along the aisles, she lost him in cosmetics. Because she gave him credit for having good sense, Sterling figured the young man would be waiting outside the store.

She took the elevator to the third floor. In Better Dresses, she found something chic that fit. The price was a little high, but she intended to charge Miss Abernathy for it as a disguise. She tied her hair into a short ponytail and wore her new green minidress out of the store, carrying her suit in a G. Fox bag.

Her young shadow waited in front of the store, but Sterling looked different when she came out of the far door. She also walked with a couple women who also carried G. Fox bags. Her poor follower never noticed she was gone.

Who would have her followed? That answer was easy. Why Alice Tower would do such a thing was trickier.

After meeting with Sterling and Miss Abernathy, Gray spent much of his day walking the streets in the North End, asking careful questions about schools, where to get scholarships, and who had connections at the school board. When he stopped at a market, he saw a stack of notices about a meeting at 6 p.m. at Missionary Apostolic Church to protest the school superintendent. He stuffed one in his pocket.

When Gray drove into the parking lot of Missionary Apostolic Church, the grounds were alive with young workers. They mowed, raked, planted flowers, even painted a fence. He stopped the nearest one to ask where the meeting was and made small talk.

Gray learned the fellow's name, college, and where he got his scholarship, moved on to the next worker, then the next.

In the shade of the church Gray scribbled what he'd learned into a small notebook and tucked it in his inside jacket pocket. On his way to Missionary Hall for the meeting, he heard an off-key rendition of "Jesus Loves Me." He bent to peek in a side basement window to see college-age women leading a group of toddlers in song.

"Can I help you?"

Gray straightened to find three youths. One had his arms folded. Two others clenched both fists.

"I'm going to the superintendent meeting," Gray said.

"You're early," said a young man wearing University of Connecticut T-shirt.

"UConn, huh? I'm a Yale man." Gray said.

"Yale man oughtta be smart enough to know he's two hours early for a meeting," snarled the UConn student.

"We'll escort you to your car," one student said. "Pastor Burundi doesn't want Bible School disturbed."

"I believe I can find my way." Gray turned and walked toward the gravel parking lot. When he reached his car, he waved to the trio.

Someone grabbed him as he dug in his pants pocket for car keys.

"Oh my God!" Sterling ran to put her arms around Gray as he stumbled in the office. His right eye was swollen, his mouth trailed blood, and he winced when she touched his side. She helped him to the loveseat.

"A-amateurs," Gray gasped. "Tituba w-warned me Alice and her brother had staunch supporters. Ouch, ah."

Sterling got the first aid kit out of the bottom drawer then handed Gray two aspirins and the rest of her soda to wash them down with.

"Here, let's stop the bleeding on your face." She poured alcohol on gauze then gently dabbed his cuts.

"Ouch! Sterling! Let me do it. You're a terrible nurse."

"I never aspired to nursing," she said. "Did you get anything for this beating?"

"M-more names of Civic Project students." He winced as he reached in his pocket.

Even for someone accustomed to reading Gray's scrawl, the names were barely decipherable. They were familiar, however.

"Why has no one noticed?" Sterling said. "The privately-funded Civic Project and publicly-funded board Community Program recipients are the same. What is the Project doing with all the donation money?"

"P-perhaps the Project supports board scholarship w-winners in other ways." Gray suggested.

"Then why not say so? Why have me followed, and all the secrecy, and this…" She looked at Gray. "Oh, leave your keys. I'm driving you home right now."

Late the next morning Gray called, sounding like his old self.

"Tituba says her grandson Jonah will talk to us. I'll come in—"

"Gray, I can handle this today," Sterling interrupted. Her partner tended to overdo. "Rest."

When she said good-bye, she called a list of colleges to speak with people in their financial offices. Next, she asked for anyone who worked with minority students who struggled academically. Then she called Miss Abernathy's brother-in-law on the school board to ask if the board's Program audit found anything. Sloppy bookkeeping—so far, he said in hushed tones.

From time to time, she chanted: "Board Funds Program, Private Funds Project." It was a way to keep things straight as she called the students and their parents.

"I wrote thank-you notes to the Civic Project and the Community Program," said a student Sterling located on the UConn campus. "I figured the money I got came from both. I got a letter from both congratulating me on my scholarship."

By late afternoon Sterling not only had a crick in her neck from cradling the phone, but she had answers about the non-profit Civic Project and board's Community Program. The whole scam angered and saddened her.

Now what? She wished for Gray

On cue Gray walked in, looking as though a fist had never touched him. An aroma like rancid horse manure followed.

"Holy Mother of God!"

"I know." Gray wore a sheepish grin. "The cab driver made me walk the last three blocks. It's Tituba's potion. She brought this nasty salve over last night and a sweet —"

"Witches' cake?"

"—buttery pound cake," Gray continued. "Good too. I know this potion stinks but even my black eye faded."

Sterling held her nose. "Potion?"

"Oh, don't worry about being attacked. Tituba put protective spells over our apartments and office."

"I'm so relieved."

"She cursed Alice Tower with a toothache or houseful of spiders. I'm not clear which."

"Spiders, I hope," Sterling said.

"And she conjured a spell to render Preacher Burundi mute," Gray said. "If she pulls that off, I'm a believer."

Sterling chuckled. "Listen to what I learned. Ah, sit over there. No, further."

When she finished reporting, Gray said, "Well, we can't announce this scholarship scheme. Who would believe us? Tituba won't tell people. The students are afraid. The Junior League can't, and the school superintendent is already facing protests for auditing a board program he supervises. In fact, there's a big march planned for Monday afternoon at the administration building on High Street."

"The con is so brazen!" Sterling fumed, paced a minute then stopped. "I've got an idea."

As she explained Gray closed his eyes. "Hm-m. We have to get Alice Tower—and anyone else who might alert her brother—out of the board building."

"Doesn't Tituba's sister work there?" Sterling said.

Gray nodded. "We have to make a lot of calls."

"Well then, why don't you go use your home phone?" Sterling gave him a wicked smile, reached in the desk drawer, and tossed him some keys. "Your car is parked where you left it."

Tituba's grandson Jonah Mitchell popped his knuckles. He and Gray waited in the large hallway outside the superintendent's office on the following Monday. "She's late. Do you think Micah's coming?"

The young man paced. Micah was his friend, a co-worker at the Missionary Apostolic Church.

"There she is." Jonah's shoulders relaxed.

Not only had she arrived, but Micah brought a friend. Gray explained what the students had to do—and couldn't do.

"We don't have time to explain how Mrs. Tower and her brother coerced you into working for her and for his church. We can't do that today. We can't say they used Civic Project money for themselves because we can't prove it," Gray told the students. "We have to nail them for what we know today. Excuse me."

A square-shouldered Black man with gray dotting his hair stepped in a front door, looked down the hallway, adjusted the jacket of his three-piece suit, then smiled at Gray. They shook hands as Sterling lead two young Black women in through a side door. She waved at Miss Abernathy from Avon, who entered through the front door.

Gray took Sterling aside. "Alice left half an hour ago for an appointment that was on her calendar. The superintendent's secretary called in sick—I have no idea how that was arranged. Tituba's sister who works here sent another Project ally to inspect a school. We have students here already." He nodded in their direction.

"I picked up two Program mothers." Sterling nodded at the man with white in his hair. "I see the president of the NAACP came."

Down the hall a wooden office door slammed so hard glass windows in the hall rattled. The racket announced three Black women followed by Tituba. The women made for Sterling and the group at the front doors.

Sterling counted thirteen people crazy enough to believe in the plan she and Gray had conjured up. An unlucky number, but just enough, she hoped, to pull off a little magic.

"We have what we need." It was as though Tituba read Sterling's mind. "And, child, stop feeling bad these kids cain't get no money from Civic Project. Things ain't over."

"The police may shake something loose," Gray said.

Tituba rattled her necklace of silver charms and mumbled, "They meant to kill my great-great-granny at the Salem witch trials, but the first Tituba was smart—and she lived."

Something about Tituba made Sterling's heart race. She motioned for Sterling to lean closer.

"I read the oracle cards…and asked around a bit. They's a safe hid in a Project's coat closet," Tituba whispered.

Sterling grinned to imagine what such a safe held. "We have to break Alice and her brother today."

"Our line of people must hold together," Gray muttered.

Tituba stuck out her bottom lip. "It'll hold. I pointed a bone at 'em."

The crowd of protesters swelled with each block they marched from Missionary Apostolic to the school board. The summer heat off the streets and in the air seemed to fuel the marchers' anger. The TV cameras turned on them, and the protesters waved cardboard signs and chanted war cries against the superintendent.

When they reached the High Street offices, Burundi mounted the first step to speak. Suddenly both double front doors whooshed open, shocking the crowd into momentary silence.

Jonah held a microphone as he walked forward shouting, "Hey, hey there. I'm Jonah Mitchell, and I thought I won a Civic Project Scholarship. Turns out I didn't get a dime from them. It all came from the Community Scholarship Program."

"Me too," Micah said into a microphone she carried. She had moved quickly to set up a stand behind Jonah, while the mother of a student set up another microphone. Others from the school board hallway waited to line up behind them.

"The school board's Program gave me a scholarship to Central Connecticut State," Micah cried. "I thought the scholarship came from the Project. I checked with school. It didn't."

"No! That's not right." A man in a jean jacket climbed two steps until Jonah stopped him.

A couple of marchers booed.

"I know it's hard truth," called Micah's friend through another microphone. "My brothers and sisters, it's hard to hear. I'm Darrell Lee, and I thought I got a Civic Project Scholarship. But all I got was money from the school board."

"That was Project money." Burundi forgot to turn on his bullhorn, so his words were drowned out by crowd's.

"You oughtta thank Pastor Burundi." A man in a faded white shirt shook his fist at Darrell.

Tituba thundered. "We've been fooled!"

"Lies!" shouted a protester's voice.

"Come say that in my face." Tituba took a half-step forward. The crowd stilled.

A high-pitched, squeal-screech marked Pastor Burundi's next failed attempt to use the bullhorn.

"Burundi can't be heard." Sterling remarked from the driver's seat of her car. She had parked in the board lot under a tree. She was close enough to hear some of the rally, but far enough away to avoid being seen.

"A lie! They…" Burundi shouted. He must have forgotten to turn on his bullhorn, so the rest of his words were lost.

"He's, ah, speechless." Gray observed from Sterling's passenger seat as he watched the next speaker take the mic.

"Listen up! I'm Diana Thompson. My son graduated from Weaver High, and he got a Program scholarship—not a penny from Project like we thought." She pointed at Burundi. "That's God's truth!"

The next speaker, the president of Connecticut Insurance, said his company gave to the Civic Project, but his staff called every college with board Program scholars and discovered none received Project money. He handed the microphone to Miss Abernathy who said she wouldn't give Junior League money to any program that wouldn't provide the simplest information like a treasurer's report. Next, the University of Hartford bursar told the crowd his school received no Project money for students — not even for tutoring help or room and board.

Murmurs in the crowd changed to angry mutters.

Suddenly Alice Tower appeared from the edge of the crowd and climbed the stairs. Her right jaw appeared swollen, her mouth sounded full of cotton.

"Dat is not true," she shouted. "Dey waited 'til I left for a dentist appointment to pull dis."

"Didn't you mention Tituba cursed Alice with a toothache?" Sterling said to her passenger.

"I thought it was spiders," Gray said.

Burundi managed to say, "My sister's being framed—" before a sneezing fit grabbed him

"I see some people who worked bake sales and car washes for the Project. Where's that money?" the president of the NAACP shouted through his microphone. "All the money to send our students to college came from the Community Program. What happened to the money we raised for the Civic Project?"

"Lies..." Burundi's shout dissolved into another series of sneezes.

Micah and Jonah began a battle cry: "Where's our money? Where's our money?"

Someone in the crowd took it up, then another person. Alice fled. Her brother followed.

"That was some powerful magic." Sterling sat, spellbound.

"It's people power," Gray scoffed. "There's power when people stand together against bullies."

"I wonder..." Sterling's voice held a touch of awe. "I wonder if Alice Tower will find a spider infestation at home."

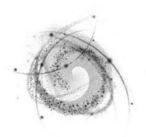

ABOUT THE AUTHOR

Water aerobics enthusiast and amateur jewelry-maker Jackie Ross Flaum is a former Hartford, CT. newspaper reporter and Memphis, TN. public relations free-lancer. Her short stories can be found in *Low Down Dirty Vote II* and *VIII, Mystery, Crime, and Mayhem, Elmwood Stories to Die For, Mayhem in Memphis, Lies Along the Mississippi,* and an upcoming *Black Cat Mystery Magazine.* Her novella *The Yellow Fever Revenge* tells of love and murder in another time of American epidemic. Short stories appearing in *Now There Was a Story, a Musical Crime Anthology* and *Modern Magic* anthology feature young detectives Madeline Sterling and Socrates Gray from her novel, *Justice Tomorrow.* She is vice president of Malice in Memphis a Killer Writing Group. Visit her website www.jrflaum.com, @jrflaum on Twitter, WriterJackieRossFlaum on Facebook, and jrflaum on Instagram.

COFFEE BREAK

BY
W.O. HEMSATH

COFFEE BREAK

S<small>*orry, I was inflating balloons.*</small>

Despite being the truth, Jess couldn't show up late to the second week of work and give Mr. Cardon that excuse. She'd heard stories of his intolerance. On a scale of one to "you're fired!" the truth was a solid eleven.

Jess licked her thumb and rubbed at some blue and pink paint flecks on her hand while maneuvering the car through morning traffic. Maybe the balloons and hand-painted banners were a touch excessive, but after two weeks on the rig, Troy was finally coming home tonight. Everything had to be perfect; she'd only get one shot to tell her new husband he was going be a dad for the first time.

Not that this was the perfect time to have a baby. After all, they'd been married a mere five weeks, and she was having a hard enough time juggling Mr. Cardon's ridiculous workload with this semester's impossible reading list. Of course, with how late she was running right now, and the unfavorable traffic report on the radio, she might not have a job to worry about much longer.

Rows of red taillights flooded the street ahead. The clock on the dash read 8:57, and she was still eight minutes away. She turned onto a side street hoping for a shortcut. Up ahead, a colorful wooden sign with a croissant and steaming coffee mug caught her eye.

Sorry, I was getting you breakfast.

Now that was a decent excuse.

As she parked, the traffic report ended and that annoying new Crenessa song started. Jess gratefully killed the engine.

Nestled between a pharmacy on the corner and a small stationery store, the coffee shop had no windows or words anywhere, not even the name of the shop. It was simply a few feet of brick walls, a faded door, and the brightly painted picture sign.

The peculiarity of it gave her a sense of apprehension, but she shook the feeling off as she grabbed her purse, locked the car, and hurried down the sidewalk. There wasn't time to waste looking for anything else.

As she reached the café, a teenager came around the corner on his bike, riding on the sidewalk.

"Sidewalks are for pedestrians," she called. "Get in the bike lane."

He kept coming toward her with a challenge in his eye and swerved around her, way too close to comfort.

She pivoted toward him in a huff, her hand protectively covering her abdomen. "You're going to hurt someone!"

The kid laughed and made a gesture behind him which her child would never be allowed to make. Jess's cheeks burned with righteous motherly indignation as she yelled after him again.

"And wear a helmet!"

More laughter, almost maniacal, erupted behind her. Two more teens on bikes raced around the corner of the pharmacy, heading straight for her. Forget reprimands; she barely had time to pull on the shop's door and duck inside before they reached her.

As the door shut behind her, the outside world fell unnaturally silent. Instead, a calming soundtrack imbued the air with sounds of wind chimes, rustling leaves, and a distant stream. The transformation of ambience was so startling, she couldn't help but sigh. Then the smells hit—warm tones of coffee, vanilla, and something that tasted like Christmas. She couldn't inhale deeply enough, but as she tried, all her anger and annoyance at the kids on bikes diffused and wafted away, as if carried on some unfelt breeze.

While not as bright as outside, the space was surprisingly well-lit for having no windows. It wasn't a harsh fluorescent light either, but a soothing, pleasant one that felt almost like early morning sunshine.

There was no one else in the shop, but a long, padded bench with pillows lined the wall clear to the back of the store. Jess followed the length of it past a few small bistro tables toward a display counter filled with Danishes, donuts, and other carb-laden delights.

As she studied the pastries, a woman appeared from a back room wearing a badge with the name *Samaya*. The woman hesitated for a moment when she saw Jess and then wiped her hands on her apron and gave a welcoming nod.

"Morning. What'll it be?"

Everything looked and sounded promising, but Jess had no idea what Cardon liked.

Cardon. Crap. How had she forgotten what a hurry she was in? Why had she wasted time yelling at those teens and soaking in the ambiance?

Jess yanked her wallet out of her purse and scanned the display case again. The safest bet was to order a variety.

"I'm in a bit of a rush, so just give me three larges of your best blends and three pastries, whichever you recommend."

The barista nodded and started on the drinks.

"Actually, make it a half dozen pastries," Jess added, silently praying Cardon could be bought off with baked goods and caffeine.

Samaya opened the back of the display case and loaded up a paper sack. When she stepped over to the register and rang up the order, Jess's hand seized around her credit card. The total was staggering.

Samaya offered a sympathetic smile and gestured toward the bench. "You really should enjoy your meal here. The experience is half of what you're paying for."

Jess surveyed the modest interior again and cocked an eyebrow at her. No amount of relaxing soundtracks or pleasant smells was worth *that* much.

Samaya shrugged. "You can walk away if the price is too steep."

For a moment, Jess considered it. Troy would flip if he saw that amount on the credit card statement. But the price of showing up late to work, empty-handed, would be even steeper. Gritting her teeth, Jess thrust her card across the counter and gathered her purchases.

Samaya handed back her card with a receipt. "Come again soon."

Fat chance that would happen. Jess hurried for the door, hands filled with her purchases. She pushed the door open with her shoulder, squinting against the change in brightness.

Wham!

Something rammed into her, knocking her against the brick storefront and making her drop everything. Coffee scalded her stomach, and she grabbed her shirt to fan it away from her skin. A tangle of wheels, limbs and ruined pastries littered the cement in front of her.

The same two teens she had narrowly dodged before entering the shop scrambled to get back on their bikes. She probably should have checked to make sure they were okay, but her coffee! Her pastries! Her shirt!

"What do you think you're doing riding laps like that? You could've killed someone," she cried, stooping to pick up her fallen things. "Slow down and get off the sidewalk!"

Looking completely freaked by her outburst, and without so much as an apology, they mounted their bikes and peeled away, leaving her with a soggy bag and brown-stained shirt. Great. Now she'd show up to work late, empty-handed, *and* un-presentable. At least when Cardon fired her, she'd have plenty of time to go home and change before picking Troy up from the airport.

No. Jess stood and faced the café. She was pregnant. She couldn't afford to lose this job and the health insurance it promised. Her benefits hadn't kicked in yet, but fifty-three more days and they would. She had to keep this job until then, whatever the cost.

She opened the door and stepped back inside, the inviting smells and sounds no longer able to wash away her frustration and urgency.

"Oh, dear," Samaya said when she saw her. "Bathroom's over here if you want to clean up. I'll get started on some replacements."

"Yes, please." Jess tossed the ruin goods into a trashcan by the door and rushed to the rear corner Samaya had gestured to.

After a couple minutes of cold water and what felt like forever under the electric hand dryer, Jess emerged from the bathroom with her blouse hopefully presentable enough to not grab Cardon's critical eye. Either way, she had to leave. At this point, she'd be almost a half hour late for work.

Samaya, bless her heart, stood outside the bathroom with a new tray of coffees and bag of pastries ready to go.

"On the house."

The tightness in Jess's chest loosened a little as she took the replacements. She didn't have the time or money to argue. "Thank you," she said, forcing herself to slow down long enough for it to seem sincere before she bolted for the door. When she reached it, she nudged it with her shoulder, checked for impending collisions, and then hurried to her car.

After securing the drinks, she turned the keys and that stupid Crenessa song started playing again. She changed the station and noticed the time on the dash said it was only 9:03.

Perfect. On top of everything else, now her car was breaking too.

Jess entered the office building with one hand clutching the pastry bag and her briefcase, the other carrying the coffees in front of her like a shield.

Cardon emerged from his office scowling, and she cringed. Exactly how late was she? Stealing a quick glance at the clock on the back wall, her heart jumped.

9:13? That had to be wrong.

Cardon zeroed in on her. "Where are yesterday's reports?"

"Right here, sir, ready to go. And I'm sorry I'm late. I was getting coffee. Take your pick." Jess handed him the tray and fumbled a stack of folders out of her briefcase while he read over the descriptions Samaya had jotted on each cup. Selecting one, he took a sip, and his eyes widened in surprise. He lowered the cup, eyed it briefly, then drew another long sip.

"Terrific brew."

The panic gripping her started to release. Cardon wasn't smiling, but he wasn't scowling anymore either. He passed back the two remaining coffees and grabbed the files from her while ogling the pastry bag. "Any bear claws?"

Jess checked the bag and beamed. Samaya had included not one but two of Cardon's favorite.

"They're both yours," she said, offering him the bag.

He tucked the files under his arm and pulled out the pastries with a satisfied grin. "You're a good addition to the team," he said, lifting his cup toward her in a toast before taking another sip and heading back to his office. "But don't be late again," he called over his shoulder. "Today's reports are on your desk."

"Of course, sir. I promise I won't—"

His door closed before she could finish, and the rest of her panic dissipated. She wasn't fired.

When she reached her cubicle, however, all her relief vanished. An impossibly large stack of papers towered next to her keyboard. They'd take all day at the office and all night at home to finish. She sank into her chair, pulled a muffin from the bag, and started in on the first report, trying hard not to think about how the drive home from the airport might be all the time she'd get to spend with Troy that night.

After a few reports, she glanced at the clock on her desk, and an uncomfortable feeling settled over her. She compared her desk clock to the one on the back office wall, the one she had assumed was wrong when she arrived. Both clocks matched.

But how? There was no way it was only 9:13 when she got to work. Given the time she left her house, the time spent in the coffee shop, and the time stuck in traffic, it should have been closer to 9:30. Could both clocks at work be broken? Maybe it was the one at home that was off.

She returned to her work, trying to be satisfied with that explanation, but no. The time in her car had matched her house clock when she left. And it matched the office clocks when she arrived. They couldn't *all* be off by the same amount of time, could they?

And what about the collision? Those kids were in the exact spot they had been in when she entered the shop. Could they really have gone around the whole block in the time she took to order and pay?

All day, there was an incessant scratching at the back of her mind, a stray thought begging to be let in, to be considered.

It was almost as if while she had been in the coffee shop, time had—

No. How could she even consider something so crazy? Was this what pregnancy hormones did to a person? Jess tried to bury herself in her reports.

But what about the song? Sure, top forty stations repeated hit songs on their playlists, but twice in fifteen minutes?

By lunch, she couldn't take it. It was the stupidest idea she'd ever had, but if she didn't prove to her silly pregnant brain that the coffee shop did not actually freeze time, she would never be able to focus enough to finish her reports. Disproving the theory would be easy; all she needed was something to throw. She filled her empty cup with water and drove with it back to the shop.

Once parked, she made sure there was no one on the street to witness her experiment and pulled the cup of water from the console. She approached the shop, opened the door, and slipped halfway in. Before she could talk herself out of it, she heaved the cup as high over the sidewalk as she could and slammed the door as fast as possible.

"What are you doing?"

Jess froze, hand on the closed door, and turned to see Samaya staring her down from the back counter.

"I . . . um . . ."

Jess searched for words to fill the silence. She couldn't bring herself to admit out loud that she thought she'd found a magic coffee shop where time stood still.

Samaya studied her for a moment, then her stern glare dropped as if it had been a mask. A smile danced behind her eyes.

"I was right. You're the new one, aren't you?"

Her current demeanor made Jess even more uncomfortable than her critical stare from moments before. The new one? What was she talking about?

"I wondered when it would pick someone else," Samaya continued. "Thought it might be you this morning, but I never know until they come back a few times. Takes most people a few visits, but you, you're quick." She laughed at Jess's bewildered face and nodded toward the door. "Well, go on. Check."

Jess's rational mind fought against the electrifying thrill of possibility that danced in the air. The way Samaya was smiling—it couldn't be, could it?

Holding her breath, she pushed on the door. The moment it cracked open, her cup and water fell, splashing at her feet.

Everything around her seemed to shift. It was impossible. It had to be impossible.

"You look like you could use a drink," Samaya's voice called from behind her. Jess turned around. Samaya was carrying two steaming mugs to one of the bistro tables. She sat down, took a drink, and patted the empty bench beside her. "Like I said before, it's best enjoyed here."

Sixty days working at Cardon's had felt like forever, especially with her frequent coffee shop visits, but her benefits had finally kicked in and not a moment too soon. Not knowing her due date, thanks to irregular cycles, was killing her. It had to be late April or early May, seeing as Troy left for the rig three weeks after the wedding, but her new OB had agreed to an ultrasound anyway to pinpoint a more specific date.

The lights in the ultrasound room were too dim to read by while she waited for the technician to begin, but Jess didn't worry anymore about reading and working in every spare moment. Closing her eyes, she gave herself permission to savor the here and now and relaxed into the padding of the reclined exam table. The disposable liner crinkled under her like tissue in a gift bag, and a faint trace of coconut hung in the air—probably the technician's lotion or something. Between the steady humming of the machines and the warm air from the vent chasing away the late October chill, the room was calm and comfortable, perfect for finally seeing her baby.

The technician's typing stopped, and the sound of her chair rolling closer on the tiled floor prompted Jess to open her eyes.

With one hand holding a bottle of gel, the technician gestured toward Jess's overstuffed bag in the corner. A textbook and file folders poked out the top.

"School or work?"

"Both," Jess said, lifting her shirt and rolling down her waistband. "Online master's and a desk job."

"Both full time?"

Jess nodded. She also wrote novels part-time, had finished three scrapbooks, and recently learned to crochet, but it didn't seem polite to brag.

The technician swirled a massive glob of clear gel onto the rounded edge of the ultrasound wand. "Where do you find time for it all?"

Jess suppressed a smirk. "I drink a lot of decaf."

"Are you sleeping enough?"

"Definitely." Eight hours every night at home, not to mention what felt like another eight hours between projects on a surprisingly comfortable café bench. She was well-rested, and for the first time in forever, she felt on top of everything. Her increased productivity had even impressed Cardon so much, rumors of a promotion floated around the office.

The one downside was she couldn't share it with Troy. That was one of the few things Samaya had explained—the shop chose one person at a time, and she was the current one. If another person was in the shop, the magic wouldn't work. It wouldn't have been such a problem, except the other rule Samaya had explained was now that Jess understood the magic and accepted it, she had to come make a purchase every day or the café would choose someone else. This meant a lot of expensive coffees, fights with Troy about credit card statements, and trying to come up with believable lies since the truth was both crazy and impossible to prove.

She hated keeping things from him, but if this one secret meant she could do, feel, and be better than she had ever been before, it was worth it. Besides, as soon as he saw the ultrasound photos of their baby, all the suspicion and tension mounting between them would melt away. Who could be upset about coffee when they were staring at their new child?

She braced herself for the cold touch of the gel, but it felt warm as the technician pressed the wand into her abdomen. The pressure against her full bladder made her wince for a moment, but the screen in front of her soon stole her focus. Different black and gray shapes morphed in and out of view as the technician slid the wand around.

Then there it was—a perfect little body with perfect kicking feet. Jess fought back tears. There would never be a moment better than this one.

The baby's legs spread apart as the technician held the wand steady with a surprised laugh. "Well, there she is." The legs kicked again. "Looks like you might have a little dancer on your hands."

Jess's breath caught in her throat. "She?"

The technician froze. "I was supposed to ask if you wanted to know the gender. I can't believe I blurted it out. That's not like me. I am so sorry."

A daughter. They were having a daughter! Jess tried to memorize every amazing detail of the little body wriggling on the screen before her. The technician still looked panicked, waiting for a response.

"It's fine," Jess reassured her. "We were planning to find out gender. I just didn't think we'd be finding it out so soon."

The technician, visibly relieved, resumed moving the wand. She clicked on the screen to record a measurement.

"Looks like it's not soon at all. You're measuring twenty weeks and two days."

The room felt suddenly cold. Jess must have heard wrong.

"I can't be more than fourteen weeks." She stared at the technician for confirmation, but the technician chuckled.

"Oh, you're definitely further along than that."

"I can't be. Measure again." There was an edge to Jess's voice now which filled the room with palpable tension.

"It's not an exact science," the technician offered. "The date could be off by a few days."

"It's off by six weeks. We didn't get married until August first."

"If you're worried people will think you got married because you were preg—"

"You don't get it." Jess's voice projected louder than she intended; it bounced off the walls of the tiny lab, but she didn't care. She needed to make this woman understand. "My husband is religious. He insisted we wait." She locked eyes with the technician. "We did."

Silence hung in the room, long and cold and awkward. The paper under Jess rustled as she waited for the technician to believe her, to acknowledge the error. The technician cleared her throat, avoiding eye contact as she resumed measuring and typing.

"I think maybe we should just finish the ultrasound. Who you share the results with—or not—will be up to you."

Jess's hands trembled as she drove to the coffee shop. She needed to make her daily purchase and come up with a plan. In her peripheral, the incriminating envelope of black and white pictures taunted her from the passenger seat.

It was ludicrous. Troy was the father. There was no way she was twenty weeks pregnant. But what could she say? That the ultrasound machine malfunctioned, and the tech was incompetent, and it only *seemed* like she cheated on him before their wedding?

She had to hide the photos and tell him a different due date. A week or two he might chalk up to error. But six weeks? Six weeks might as well be forever. It was almost as long as she'd been working for Cardon. Almost as long since she discovered the coffee shop.

A cold idea bit the edges of her mind, and her chest tightened.

The coffee shop.

If she estimated ten hours working on projects and eight hours sleeping on the bench, seven days a week, for eight weeks—

Her knuckles whitened as she clung to the steering wheel. It added up to six full weeks.

A few broken speed limits, a crooked parking job, and some thunderous steps later, Jess barged into the patron-less cafe. Samaya stood at the back, drying a mug.

"You lied!" Jess pointed an accusatory finger at her as she marched back to the counter. "I wasn't getting extra time."

Samaya raised a challenging eyebrow but continued drying. "There's no such thing as extra time. I never said there was."

"But all this time I've been in here working—day after day, week after week—you let me think time was standing still."

"It is." Samaya jutted her chin toward the door. "Outside."

How could she stand there, drying that stupid mug, not realizing what a huge problem she'd created? Jess slapped the counter with her palm. Samaya didn't flinch.

"You never told me I was still aging. That *my baby* was still aging. You never told me I was stealing from our future."

"You're right." Samaya set the mug down and whipped the dish towel over her shoulder. "I simply said you can walk away if the price is too steep, and that if you do, it'll choose someone else."

An uncharacteristic hardness fell over Samaya's features. Jess took a step back as realization set in. Samaya would not be giving her any kind of apology or solution; she was giving her an ultimatum.

Keep using the coffee shop or walk away forever.

Jess turned to the familiar bench stretching out before her, empty and inviting. Every moment she stayed would cost her future and possibly her marriage, if she hadn't lost it already. But without the shop, she'd never finish her degree or novel, let alone keep up with work and sleep. Cardon would never give her that promotion once her productivity dropped. Troy would be upset when she failed classes they couldn't afford for her to retake. This shop had made all her dreams possible. How could she walk away from the most miraculous thing she'd ever had?

Samaya's voice, cold and curt, pierced her thoughts. "Are you going to order or not?"

As Jess agonized over the impossibility of her choice and the injustice of it all, her stomach fluttered. She tried to will the anxiety away and fought back hot tears, refusing to cry in front of Samaya.

Her stomach fluttered again.

And again.

Serenity washed over her as she realized the flutters weren't anxiety. They were her daughter—moving, stretching, growing. Jess marveled at the sensation. It felt…magical.

Resting a hand on her stomach where her daughter had kicked, Jess drew in a deep breath and met Samaya's expectant stare. In that moment, she knew there really wasn't a choice at all.

Without another word, Jess turned and exited the shop. From that moment on, the only magic that mattered was the one growing inside her.

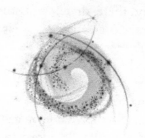

ABOUT THE AUTHOR

W.O. Hemsath is the mother of four boys and considers herself blessed to be married to her best friend. She currently lives in Minnesota, but has also lived in Utah, Arizona, California, Argentina, and New Zealand. She loves traveling, cardio dance, watching movies with a bowl of ice cream, and really good back scratches. She has a degree in screenwriting, enjoys teaching at writing conferences, and generally writes stories with a touch of magic, mystery, or aliens. To see what she's written or what she's currently up to, find her online at any of the links below:

Twitter: @WhitneyHemsath

Facebook: @AuthorWhitneyHemsath

Website: whitneyhemsath.wordpress.com

ABOUT THE AUTHOR

FORTUNES
BY
MONICA WENZEL

FORTUNES

At the only occupied table in Zhao's Zen Asian Kitchen, Kristy smiled for the first time that night. For the first time in several weeks. Not the smile she put on her face to make her friend Jess worry less and help them enjoy the dinner, but an actual smile.

Kristy ate the last few noodles of her chicken lo mien. She'd planned on saving half of it for lunch at work tomorrow, but it tasted too good to leave any tonight. Only two small pieces of broccoli and a few grains of rice sat on Jess's plate of beef and broccoli.

"I needed this. And not just this." She pointed her chopsticks at her empty plate. "Thanks for inviting me out."

"I've had a good time, too. We should do this more than once a month."

"I'd need an actual raise for that. Not what my manager called a raise during my performance review."

"You need a new job."

"I need a new life."

Benjamin Zhao set the check and two fortune cookies down between Kristy and Jess.

"No rush, ladies. Drink more tea. Eat your cookies. Talk as long as you want. It's not like I have a line of customers waiting to sit down."

"We're going to come back again for sure. That food was so good it's magical," Kristy said.

Benjamin gave her an awkward smile.

"She means it," Jess said. "There's something about those scallion pancakes that's closer to a religious experience than just food. Our compliments to the chef."

Benjamin took a theatrical bow.

"Really? You serve tables after you cook the food for them? Do you mop your own floors, too?"

"This is my place. I love every minute I'm here, even the ones where I'm cleaning the tables. I could've been a doctor. I was studying for it, but it wasn't just right for me."

"That's quite the shift in careers," Kristy said.

"It's just a different form of caring for people. I'm better at making people's mouths water than diagnosing their sore throats. I've always loved cooking with my mother and grandmother. They taught me everything I know about being in the kitchen."

"My stomach thanks them," Kristy said, patting it.

"So, no wife to help out here or go home to?" Jess gave him a smile.

"Not yet. Maybe one day, but for now I'm enjoying my life here. It's as close to a calling as I've ever gotten for a career. Enjoy your fortune cookies. I make them myself."

"That doesn't surprise me," Jess said.

Benjamin cleared the empty plates and brought them back to the kitchen. Probably to wash them himself, Kristy thought.

Jess cracked her fortune cookie and read the paper inside.

"Other people rely on you."

"In bed," Kristy added.

The friends laughed.

"Good thing the food is better than the fortunes here."

"I've had worse fortunes. Like the one that said I'll be hungry an hour later. Or the one that told me to not worry about money because the best things in life are free."

"I got one that told me to pick another cookie once. What does yours say?"

Kristy ate her cookie and opened the paper inside, as was her habit when eating fortune cookies. She turned it over, but she still saw blank paper.

"Great. I got a blank fortune. It's like the universe is trying to tell me something."

She tossed it next to her plate. Jess picked it up and rummaged through her purse for a pen.

"Let's write your own. What do you want? A raise? A date with a good man?"

"I don't need a date. I can always trip a guy like my grandma told me to."

Jess laughed. "I forgot about that. She told you to—"

"Walk down the street and trip a guy. Maybe we should write the fortune to have a guy fall for me soon."

Pots clanged in the kitchen and Benjamin raced out.

"Stop! Don't write anything."

"It's just a blank fortune."

"Exactly. It's a blank fortune. Anything you write on there will come true."

Kristy raised her eyebrows at him.

"I promise. I don't know how, but every time someone gets a blank fortune at my restaurant, it is exactly when they need it the most."

"It's like the magic you put in the food," Jess said.

"I'm still learning exactly how my magic works, but yes, the magic that helped me built this restaurant knows how and what people need more than I do."

"We were joking earlier about the magic in the food," Jess said.

"I wasn't," Benjamin said.

He looked serious enough for Jess and Kristy to believe him.

"Think about it first. Make sure what you write on there is what you want and need most."

"So, a rent-free condo is out of the question?" Jess asked.

Benjamin thought for a second. "Not necessarily, if it's what you want the most in life. You won't ever get this chance again. Not even if you live to be over one hundred. Make the most of this chance."

"This must happen every day for one of your customers," Jess said.

"A few times a year at most, and only if someone really needs it. I promise it will come true if it's what you need most right now, and it's something that can improve the rest of your life."

Kristy narrowed her eyes at him. "You're not joking."

"I never joke about my fortunes. They're always somehow right." He looked at Jess. "Your friend is depending on you to help her get through this hard time and not just for dinner company. She needs a real friend."

Kristy nodded her head slightly.

"Whatever we put on this paper is guaranteed to happen?" Jess said. "Whatever she needs?"

"Not exactly guaranteed. You won't get a refund on your dinners or a new blank fortune. But no one has ever come back and said the fortune didn't work. I'll give you some privacy to think about it."

Benjamin left the dining room and silence filled it. Both friends stared at the blank slip of paper for a few minutes.

"So, what do you actually want the most?" Jess asked.

Kristy opened her mouth and shut it. She thought about a townhouse that was already paid for. She wasn't sure how she'd explain that to anyone who asked, not that she felt the need to explain her finances. She considered wishing for a good man who was interested in her, but she'd always feel unsure if his attraction was authentic or just created by the wish. Wishing for a new job was tempting, but also temporary compared to the rest of her life.

She turned the slip of paper over and over in her fingers. Jess handed her the pen.

"Make a good choice. This is your future."

Kristy took a deep breath and wrote a sentence on the paper. Immediately, her smile got wider.

Benjamin came back out of the kitchen to finish payment and check up on the fortune. He nodded when he read it.

"Good choice."

"I thought so. Obviously," Kristy said.

"You probably have lots of questions," he said.

She had two that she really wanted answered.

"What does your magic give you?"

Benjamin waved a hand around the restaurant. "It gives me enough money each month to keep this place running and me doing what I enjoy. I won't ever get rich, but I'll always have enough."

"And you think the magic will work for me? Really work?" She tried not to sound as pathetic and desperate for something good in her life as she felt.

Benjamin nodded. "It wouldn't give you a blank fortune if it didn't think you needed one in your life right now."

She was tempted to ask about how the magic worked, or how he developed it, or if it ran in his family. But she decided that none of those were really important if her fortune worked.

"I'll come back and tell you how the fortune went."

"I look forward to it."

Kristy slipped into her jacket and headed for the door not fully expecting her new fortune to come true. At least she felt better than she had when she'd entered Benjamin's restaurant.

When she woke up in the morning, her good mood continued. She thought it was lingering effects of spending an evening with one of her best friends from college. As the day turned into a week, and the week stretched on into two, and then three, and then a month, she had to admit to herself that the continuing good feeling wasn't an accident.

"Happiness follows you all the days of your life."

The sentence had barely fit on the blank slip of paper. It had certainly fit itself into her life now.

The next time she went back to the restaurant, she'd have to tell Benjamin about her life lately. She wasn't sure exactly what she'd tell him. She didn't have anything concrete to talk to him about, like a new boyfriend, or a job promotion, or a larger and better apartment. But she felt noticeably and consistently happier.

Maybe it was just an idea planted in her head that she made real through her thoughts. Maybe Benjamin had some real talent besides cooking delicious food. She'd spend the rest of her life wondering exactly what happened. For the moment, the increased happiness was more than enough for her to believe that her blank fortune had come true.

ABOUT THE AUTHOR

Monica teaches high school Spanish during the day and writes at night and on the weekends. She'd like to thank coffee for letting her keep up with all of her responsibilities.

She's also learned and taught French. Her first professional job was teaching high school English in rural Ecuador where she was one of three people in the town of 1,000 who could speak English well enough to have a conversation. Now she lives in Minnesota with her husband, son, and two cats.

In addition to writing and speaking multiple languages, she enjoys photography, going to the park or on bike rides with her family, and traveling. She's visited France, Spain, Germany, England, China, South Korea, and many states. Her stories have been previously published in the anthologies *On Time* and *Wayward Fables*, and the online magazines *Every Day Fiction*, *101 Words*, and *Enchanted Conversation*.

Her instagram is @monicawenzel8.

DEALER'S CHOICE
BY
MANFRED GABRIEL

DEALER'S CHOICE

Place your bet and find the lady, five will get you ten, ten will get you twenty, twenty will get you forty." Demetri spoke rapid fire, a sideshow barker in another life. As he talked, he moved three slightly bent playing cards around a makeshift cardboard table on his lap. Picking them up and dropping them in turn, the middle card to the left, the left card to the right, the right card to the middle, and then back again.

A crowd had formed around him, swaying almost as one as the L train took a wide turn. Demetri stopped his spiel as the last card was dropped. The attractive young woman in front of him, who had set down a crumpled twenty to play, pointed to the card on the right. Demetri flipped it over to reveal the queen of spades.

"The madam wins," Demetri said, smiling as if pleased to lose money. "Give me another shot?" She let it ride, playing three more times, each time picking the queen of spades, each time doubling her winnings. With each win, she squealed with delight, clapped her hands, looked around at the other passengers with a light in her blue eyes that said, "See how easy it is."

Her name was Deanna, and she was his shill. Demetri let her win to draw others into the game. They had worked together for over a year, along with Clive, who stood at the end of the car with thick, tattooed arms folded across his chest, on the lookout for the cops, or ready to intervene in case someone decided they didn't like losing.

Deanna did her job well. A boy who couldn't have been more than thirteen, wiry with wide eyes, stepped up and placed a five-dollar bill on the cardboard table. Demetri figured it was all the boy had. He took the bet, placing down his own five. He moved the cards around, a little more slowly than normal, the boy watching carefully. When the boy picked the queen of spades, the boy laughed, taking the two fives and scurrying away.

Clive would no doubt be angry with Demetri for letting the boy win. Money was money, he would say in his raspy baritone. But Demetri wasn't in the business of taking money from people who needed it more than he did.

A couple approached from across the car. The guy wore an expensive leather jacket that all but screamed, "mug me." The woman had a rock on her ring finger that must have cost ten grand, and she clung to the man's arm as if afraid of losing her gravy train. It was early evening. The downtown clubs and restaurants were starting to fill with suburbanites on their way to a show at the Roxy or the New Haven. Most drove or took ride shares, but some, like this couple, preferred the adventure of rubbing elbows with common folk.

The guy put down a fifty. Demetri shrugged, laid a ten and two twenties on top of it, then worked his magic, moving the cards as he rattled on, "Round and round the lady goes, where she stops, no one knows." Demetri ended by gesturing to the cards with an open palm.

The guy picked out the middle card, guessing right. He grinned broadly as the woman clung to him even tighter.

"Let me get the chance to break even," Demetri said.

The guy nodded. After a quick shuffle, he picked out the queen of spades again. After winning once more, three-hundred dollars were on the table. Demetri asked if the guy felt lucky. The guy said sure, a smug look on his face.

Demetri started the game again, going on a little longer than before, ending abruptly. When the guy chose the card on the right, Demetri turned it over to reveal the five of hearts. He frowned, feigning disappointment.

The guy opened his mouth to protest, but Demetri had already scooped up the cash and shoved it in his breast pocket. He looked at Clive, who tilted his head to the next car. A transit officer was heading towards them.

The train jilted to a halt. The doors slid open. Demetri took this as his cue to exit, cards and cardboard in hand.

He hurried across the platform, down the stairs, across the station and then up another set of stairs to the platform for trains heading the opposite direction. He would hop the next train and meet up with Clive and Deanna one stop over, where they would resume their hunt for new suckers.

Demetri had no remorse about taking their money. After all, they knew what they were getting into. A cursory search on the internet would tell them it was a scam. Still, they thought they could beat the game. They were sure they could beat Demetri. As if nicer clothes, a fat bank account, and an expensive phone meant they were somehow smarter than him. That since they knew the trick to it, they could find the right card. But Demetri wasn't some card shark from an old Western. He had more than an ace up his sleeve.

The days were growing longer. Though it was near dinner time, the sun still shone above the three flats and tenements, casting shadows on the downtown skyline beyond. Demetri was shielding his eyes with his hand as he looked down the tracks for the approaching train when he felt a tug on his sleeve.

He whipped around, ready to start swinging or make a run for it, depending on who was there. The man in front of him was so disarming, he did neither. He was short, not little person short, but at six foot three, Demetri towered over him. His close-cropped hair was speckled gray, his dull brown eyes seemed to have nothing going on behind them.

"Sorry to bother you," the man said. He spoke with a slight lisp and his voice was high pitched, almost that of a young girl's. "I was wondering if you could show me how you do it."

"How I do what?" Demetri said, playing dumb.

The man looked to the cardboard and cards in Demetri's hand. "We both know what I'm talking about."

"I'm just on my way home from work. Why don't you go bother someone else?"

The man shook his head. "I'm willing to pay." From the front pocket of his baggy trousers, he pulled five one-hundred-dollar bills, splayed them so that Demetri could see that they were real, real enough, anyway.

Demetri almost salivated. It was a day's take, and he wouldn't have to split it with Deanne and Clive. The man didn't resist as Demetri pocketed the money.

Sitting on a nearby bench, Demetri set the cardboard on his lap, showed the cards face up to the man—a five and six of hearts and the queen of spades.

"You can use any cards you want, but I like these for contrast." He placed the three cards in a row face down. "It helps if they're slightly bent but not creased, makes them easier to handle. You show the mark the three cards, make sure they know where the queen is. You pick up two in one hand, one in the other, you throw them down. The one in the one hand doesn't matter. The two in the other hand are what are important. When you look like you're throwing down the bottom card, you're really throwing down the top card." He demonstrated in slow motion. "Do it quick enough, and no one can tell." He sped up his movement. "The mark ends up following the wrong card."

The man crossed his arms. "I know that's how most people do it. I can get that on YouTube. My question is, how do *you* do it?"

Demetri looked down the empty tracks, anxious for a train to come. "Damn things never run on schedule," he said.

The man smiled a thin, lipless smile. "You're avoiding my question."

Demetri rose and started towards the stairs. He didn't like where this conversation was going. He would walk to the next station, or maybe hop a bus. Anything to get away from this man and questions he didn't want to answer.

The man hurried to block his path. Demetri could have easily pushed him out of the way, but worried, if this man knew so much about cards, what else did he know? He could see himself suddenly flat on his stomach with his arms pinned behind him or thrown onto the tracks as he tried to get by.

A group of teenagers appeared on the other end of the platform, chattering with one another while staring into their phones. Two boys and two girls, Asians, Vietnamese probably. The station wasn't that far from Little Saigon.

"One more time. Pretend I'm a mark," the man said. He pulled another hundred from his pocket.

Demetri shrugged, sat back down. He started to move the cards around like he had done a thousand times before, but this time without his normal spiel. The man watched carefully, and when Demetri stopped, the man casually pointed to the card on the left.

The wrong card, Demetri thought, and so he couldn't help a look of disbelief when the queen of spades turned up.

"You aren't the only one with talents," the man said as Demetri watched the hundred disappear, going nowhere in particular. "I've been watching you. Not just today on the train, but when you were working outside the ballpark yesterday, on the city mall last week. Don't be surprised you didn't see me. I can make myself easy to miss."

"I don't know how I can do what I do," Demetri said, seeing no reason to keep his secret any longer. "I started with the normal sleight of hand, but after a while, I found I didn't need it."

The man nodded. "Have you ever tried it with anything else? Maybe on the gambling riverboats, perhaps even Vegas?"

"Hit the Indian Casino once," Demetri admitted. "Lost all I had. Figured it only worked with three card monte."

"That's because you're untrained. I could help you."

"What, so I can clean up at blackjack?"

The man shook his head. "Cards aren't the only thing that can be switched—documents, money, even people."

"People?"

The man glanced sideways. Demetri followed his gaze. The four teenagers were still standing, waiting, talking, lost in their phones. Only they weren't Asian anymore, they were Hispanic.

"Don't worry," the man said. "The others aren't gone. I just shuffled them around, is all."

Demetri tried hard to grasp what he was seeing. The man must have seen the look of confusion on his face. He raised an eyebrow.

"Let's say you want to divorce your wife, but she's suing you for half of your hard-earned cash. The morning you're both set to appear in court, she's about to enter, when suddenly, she's replaced by some homeless woman off the street, or a kid from a nearby playground. Her lawyer is confused. So is the judge, but he has no choice but to throw out her claim. Afterwards, she's sitting in her car, wondering what happened, but by then it's too late."

Demetri thought a moment. "You get paid for this?"

"You'd be surprised how well. You could put your Mom and sister up somewhere nicer than that apartment you rent up on Kenmore."

Demetri didn't ask how the man knew about his family, how he had to support the three of them all by himself. Like the man had said, he'd been watching. Still, the thought of it sent a shiver down his spine. "I don't know," Demetri said. "I like what I do."

"What's that have to do with it?" The man scoffed. "You think all those seven figure portfolio managers downtown like their jobs? Hell no. They'd quit in a heartbeat if they could. We make choices in life. They made theirs. You need to make yours."

"What if I said that I'll keep to what I know?"

"Let's just say we'd be concerned, someone with your talents, a free agent. I'd hope it wouldn't come to that, though. I understand the thrill of taking advantage of someone who thought they were better than you just because they were born in a fancier house, had more money. Look at me, a little man, to some, hardly a man at all."

The teenagers were Asian again, seemingly unaware anything had changed. The platform shook slightly as the train approached.

"How do I know if they deserve what their getting?" Demetri asked.

"It can make you rich," the man said, as if this was a satisfactory answer.

Demetri thought about what his church-every-Sunday mother might say. Even now, she thought he worked as a messenger for a big law firm. Even though he'd justified what he did in his own mind, she'd never approve of what he did now, let alone approve of taking the man up on his offer.

"Thanks, but no thanks," Demetri said. He put his cards in his pocket alongside the money the man had given him.

The train arrived. Demetri boarded the nearest car, leaving the man behind. As the doors slid closed, he suddenly found himself, not in the familiar confines of an L train, with its plastic seats and tinted windows, its advertisements sprayed with graffiti, but in a small room, dimly lit with no windows, sitting in a straight, uncomfortable chair.

His hand moved to his pocket. His money was gone, but the cards were still there. He took them out. Three cards, all of them a queen of spades, scepter in one hand, flower in the other, eyes slanted, seductive, looking at him, looking beyond him, looking at the empty walls.

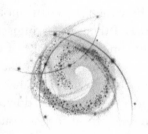

ABOUT THE AUTHOR

Manfred Gabriel works with people all day and writes evenings to keep his sanity. He has been telling stories, primarily speculative fiction, for almost 30 years. His work has appeared in over two dozen publications. He lives and writes in Western Wisconsin, where he lives with his three children and two cats who think they're dogs.

THE DRAGON PEN
BY
JULIE DAY

THE DRAGON PEN

*S*he *looked adoringly at his puppy-dog eyes*, she wrote. Ugh. Too sweet. Gushy. Katie screwed up the sheet of paper, lobbing it towards the wastepaper bin in the corner of her study. This wasn't going well, and she had a deadline to meet. What was she going to tell her editor?

She picked up another sheet, trying again, *Casey gazed loving...* What the? No! The pen couldn't run out now. She breathed on it. She shook it upside down and tried again. Still nothing. Why now? There was ink left in the pen; she could see it.

Katie rummaged in the bureau where she kept her spare stationery. One of the three pens she found had to work, surely?

Right. This needed to get done. Her editor's words to her were fresh in her mind.

"Katie, don't write to the wire, will you? Your ideas have been weaker, make this a good one, yes?"

Yes, Kate had agreed. So, now all she needed was a fantastic plot, written on time. You pens will need to work your magic.

The first one left a bubble of ink on the paper. The second one seemed fine. Until the second sentence, *Casey stroked his arm...* Double ugh! Too...twee. Weak. Not strong enough, no drama.

She picked up the third and final pen. Then put it down again. What she needed was a new pen, an inspirational pen. And some fresh air to revive her brain.

The charity shop on the corner of the High Street—they sold new stuff, stationery, pens and the like. She'd head there.

The shop was chock full of blouses, skirts, kids' clothes, jigsaws and books stacked high. Pens. Where were the pens?

"Can I help you?" A lady with long dark hair materialised beside her.

"I expect you can. A pen. That's what I'm after," Katie said. "I write romance and am on a deadline. I need inspiration. All the ones I have at home are working against me."

"I think we have exactly what you want. Follow me."

The lady pulled a box out from under the counter and offered Katie a fine selection. "This one is perfect. Here, hold it, try it, see if it feels right for you," the lady offered.

As soon as Katie touched it, she felt a fizz, like a tiny electric shock, tingling up her fingers. What was it—energy, excitement, anticipation, or all three? Her heart tap, tap, tapped. This was the pen for her.

"I'll take it," she said.

"I knew it." The lady's blue eyes shone like a twinkling sea.

Katie wanted to shake her hand in thanks, but the lady gave her wave instead, and retreated into the room behind the counter.

Back home, Katie made straight for her desk. As soon as the pen touched the paper, the words flowed. She must be tired; she rubbed her eyes. She couldn't have seen the dragon on the pen open its wings and breathe fire, could she?

The first sheet was done in no time. She began a second. Once the first words were down, there was no stopping her. The ideas bubbling in her brain had to be gotten down onto paper, or her mind would burst.

Finally, the pen stopped. Katie was exhausted. Her stomach rumbled. It couldn't be 4.30, could it? Had she been writing all that time? It had flown by.

After a brief re-fuelling break, she was back at her desk, pen in hand. She felt the same tingle she'd felt in the shop; she'd been hit by a fresh burst of energy.

Again, the words flowed like water from a kettle. It was as if the ideas went straight from her brain to the ink, then on to the paper. The fire she'd felt in her belly for her early novels was back. If only, Shirley, her editor could see her now.

She fell into bed, and immediately to sleep, no fretting over the words she'd find tomorrow.

The next day was the same. And the one after that. It seemed like no time until she was writing, *The End*. She laid the pen on her desk. The dragon slept. Its wings curled around its back. Yes, she felt like that too; wanting to curl up and sleep but she had to review her work and get it to Shirley.

This time she was pleased with what she read. Delighted, even. This would make Shirley sit up and take notice, she was sure.

She opened a new document on her computer and began typing it all up. When she reached chapter four, she attached it to an email and pressed 'send.' Then she continued the rest of the story.

That night she dreamt of dragons breathing fire. Comforting fire, encompassing her, keeping her warm and safe.

She woke late the following morning, refreshed and alert.

It was too soon to expect to have heard back from Shirley. Too early to start anything new. She'd pop into the shop and thank the lady for finding the pen for her. The last few weeks had been so busy with writing, she'd barely had a chance to leave the house.

Katie searched for the same lady with long hair. She saw ladies with short dark hair and long blonde hair but not the lady from the day before.

When she was the first one in the line, she looked at the case. No pens. Brooches, earrings, and other jewellery, but no pens. Maybe they had sold out.

"Hello," the lady behind the counter said. "How may I help you?"

"Oh, I wondered if you have another pen like this," and she took out her dragon pen.

The lady gasped. "Where did you get that pen from?"

"From here, a few weeks ago. A lady with long dark hair sold it to me. Is she not here today?"

The lady blinked. "Er, no," she replied.

"Do you have any more like this one?"

"Oh, no. We haven't sold any like that for years. Customers kept bringing them back complaining that the ink spilled and made blotches everywhere. So, we withdrew them from the shop. You say that a lady with long dark hair sold it to you?" Her eyebrows went up with the question.

Katie nodded. "She said that she believed it was perfect for me, being a romance writer."

"Ah, that does explain something to me. Hold on, I just want to get something to show you."

Katie waited.

A minute later the lady returned with a photo. "Was this the lady you saw?"

Katie looked at the photo of a woman with long dark hair and sparkling blue eyes. "Yes. Who is it?"

"That was my late aunt. She founded the shop and was a writer, too. She also loved pens, and had an affinity with other writers, especially romance ones. She sensed when they needed help. Did you?"

"Yes, I got blocked and had lost my motivation."

The lady beamed at her. "So pleased it helped. You can keep the pen. I'm sure Aunt Belinda would like that, as she did choose it for you."

"Where is your aunt? I'd like to thank her." Katie glanced round the shop and to the back where saw another lady lifting a bag.

"She died a few years ago and left the shop to me." Katie saw a tear trickle down the lady's cheek.

"I'm sorry to hear that. I hoped I haven't upset you," Katie said.

"You haven't, don't worry. It's just that it's been ages since someone has come here and said that they saw Aunt Belinda here. Is there anything else I can help with?"

"No, you've helped all you can. Thank you." Katie dashed out of the shop.

Back home, Katie sat at her desk. She thought about what the lady said. Oh my, that meant she had seen a ghost, one that was a fellow writer.

She took out her pen. "Thank you, Belinda." She blinked as she was sure she saw smoke coming out of the nib, then heard a sigh like the dragon was now content.

She began writing. After a couple of words, the ink ran out. Oh no! Now what did she do?

She glanced at the dragon. Maybe it hadn't been the tool that inspired her to write but the picture of the dragon there.

That night, as she drifted into slumber, Katie thought she heard a voice she recognised. It sounded like the lady from the shop. She said to her, "Well done, Katie, on finishing the novel. And for realising it wasn't the pen that gave you the idea but the dragon who inspired you. Think about it. Good luck."

When Katie woke up the next morning, those words stayed in her mind.

As she passed her desk and the pen, her fingers twitched as though they had sensed the pen. First, she had to find out what Shirley thought of the book.

She logged on to her emails. Yep, there was a reply. She took a deep breath, then clicked on it.

Katie let out her breath. She read, "You've got the fire back, Katie. I stayed up all night to read it. They will love it. More please."

Katie searched around for an object or picture to inspire her. The pen and its dragon caught her eye. Yes, that's what had been lacking—her heroine needed more fire in her. She had also needed fire in her writing and had been lost for ages. Now she had it back.

She said, "Thank you, Belinda, for getting me to see the light. You gave me the heat to get back my fire to write like I used to. I'll dedicate the book to you when it's published."

The dragon on the pen appeared to wink at her then went back to sleep. She chuckled, "And thank you, dragon."

ABOUT THE AUTHOR

Julie Day lives in SE London, UK. Julie has Asperger's Syndrome. She is an indie author of the children's series 'The Rainbow School' about autistic children finding confidence at school via magical elements. She also writes for adults about helpful ghosts, (especially ancestors helping relatives as in her 'Geraldine's Gem's' series), short stories and magazine fillers. She is currently writing a second children's series featuring autistic children, and her first cozy mystery with a helpful ghost. She has recently published her memoir about having endocarditis. You can connect with her online:

http://www.twitter.com/@juliedayauthor
http://facebook.com/AuthorJulieDay
My website: http://www.julieaday.co.uk
My blog: http://www.julieaday.blogspot.com

WINDOW
BY
DARREN TODD

WINDOW

I'm not suggesting I went through. It was dark. I'd been drinking. Did I experience two places? Sure. But so does a New York City tourist walking through Little Italy who stumbles into Chinatown.

It played out subtler than that, of course. Fenster, Germany and Fenster, Arizona share obvious Germanic influences. I didn't wander into a Brazilian slum or a settlement of Nepalese yurts. Even if I'd met someone on the other side, both towns are primarily Jewish, sprinkled with gentile tourists. A cold winter for Arizona matched a late one for Germany. A few months sooner or later, weeks even, and just the weather would have discredited what happened. Or validated it, I suppose.

Either way, I saw enough to make publishing the article dubious. So not only did I ruin a once-in-a-generation phenomenon, I had to trash my piece. A month's worth of work. I'm not the most well-known writer in the biz, so journalistic integrity is sometimes all I have. I could honestly claim that I'd found nothing to vet the portal and Fenster's kitsch history until that night.

In a way, I wish some hack writer would have experienced it. The kind who claims they "felt something" while on the hour-long historical tour and has the nerve to spill enough ink for a twenty-inch article. They'd have pubbed in some glam rag between celebrity rehab photo spreads, and the world would have forgotten about it by the next issue.

My target magazine wanted a particular version of events. Certainly the version I had expected to write and had constructed in the month leading up to that night. Let's call it "calculated condemnation." The kind that wears a loose veil of receptiveness. I had it all but written, perhaps another round of edits, another day of fact-checking, and I'd have exchanged those ten-thousand words for three-thousand dollars. I sacrificed a paycheck *and* my reputation when I buried it.

Did I admit my reasons to the editor? Did I call up the editor-in-chief of *American Skeptic* and say I'd seen the portal? That I'd passed through it? What, and never publish investigative journalism again?

No. I took the hit to my bank account and my pride, and I tucked that night into my back pocket when I left.

So, about that night. I'd finished the latest round of interviews with the mayor and his wife earlier that day. Separately, of course. They corroborated most of the claims people made, maybe a little too well. Later on, I changed into some casual clothes, left my recorder in the room, and had a few drinks with the mayor's wife. We toasted the end of the article. I'm sure they were both as excited as I was to wrap it up.

"Mr. Avery," she said, holding up her Cosmopolitan. "We are so happy to have had your company these last weeks. The writers, they come and go. No one really wants the full story about the window. They want the sound bite," she said and chuckled. She spoke with a sort of high society, even elderly affectation, despite being on the better side of forty.

"My sentiments exactly, Mrs. Mayor." She liked it when I called her that. "I'm not interested in the CliffsNotes version. Readers are sick of paragraph-long 'stories' whether they know it or not. The portal deserves more than that."

Sure, I laid it on thick. We'd exchanged such back-patting near the beginning of my stay, but I'd have no chance to speak to her again. My recorder held a good ten hours of audio from my visits to the mayor's so-called mansion. Mostly just another house close to city center and the supposed location of the portal. But I was hoping the desire to unload and let her guard drop a little—oiled by alcohol—might furnish me with one last quote.

"Mr. Avery. Bradley," she said, closing her eyes as if conjuring an old memory. "I know you've searched for the truth. As dedicated as you've been to this story, I think you deserve it."

I kept quiet. People are so desperate to fill conversational voids, all a reporter has to do is keep his damned mouth shut and the story will come out eventually. The bar of the Fenster B&B seemed as good a place as any. Tourists sat interspersed with small pockets of locals drinking in twos and threes. The swell of talking and soft music covered our conversation but still let us speak in low tones without leaning close in shared conspiracy.

"The last time the portal opened was during the war, right? The Jews used it to escape Nazi invasion. Including my grandmother-in-law, God rest her soul." She closed her eyes again, smiled, and bobbed her head like it was dangling from a bungee cord. "A great story. You've heard it from every angle by now. The portal saved more Jews than Schindler. Wonderful idea." She leaned in closer, even looked to her left and right as if her husband or a town elder might be waiting for her to slip up. "Don't you think it's a little... convenient? I mean, there's no better time for it to have opened. If... if it's true. But we've had our eyes on that spot in the cobblestones for the last twenty years, guarding it like Buckingham Palace, and it's not so much as rippled. I mean, there's a reason they did a movie about Schindler but not about Fenster, right?

I shrugged. "I've seen several documentaries about Fenster, though. Wouldn't have known Schindler's name if not for the film."

She pursed her lips in thought. "'Documentaries' is being nice. There are just as many 'documentaries' on Bigfoot."

"Fair enough," I said.

She shrugged. "Granted, half the town is Jewish, and this part of the state has an atypical number of them. Even if many of them followed the money and the jobs right out of Fenster, like anyone would. But whether they came through the portal or rode a pack mule, what would it have been like if they'd never come?"

"I'm not sure I follow you, Mrs. Mayor."

"You know your history, I'm assuming. We like to look back and wag our finger at Germany for what happened while the rest of us sit on our high horses, absolved of wrongdoing."

I nodded. "Sure, at the same time millions of Russians were starving and China lost, like, fifteen million—"

She shook her head. "No, I'm talking about the Jews specifically. Ask people nowadays, even some Jews, and you'd think Hitler struck like a snake."

"Right."

"But that madman told the United States, along with every other nation crying foul, that if they wanted Jews, he'd be more than willing to hand them over. How many did they want?" She made a gesture like she was proffering hors d'oeuvres.

"And you're telling me Fenster, Arizona didn't say: 'We'll take two thousand.'"

She dipped forward, grinning at the joke. "Exactly. So, who knows how things would be different. God knows there wouldn't be a democrat sheriff in Maricopa County without Jewish backing. We could still be suffering under that whack-o that won back in '93. The one who wanted to feed all the prisoners spoiled food and make them wear pink underwear to humiliate them. He put up those tents in the desert to hold the jail overflow."

"Tent city. I remember. Sheriff Huxley tore it down in '96."

"You know what he called it? What the whack-o called those tents?"

I shrugged.

"A concentration camp. Even bragged about it. Who knows the suffering a guy like that would have wrought."

I took a drink from my beer but kept quiet.

"But I get it. For every Jew in Fenster who swears up and down they came from Germany—poured through the window with all the others—you've got another who remembers some harrowing journey across the country to get here."

In Fenster, any narrative about immigrating that *didn't* involve the portal fell into a scalpel-wide minority. Despite my blood-hounding, I'd uncovered maybe two. And yet deep, rich stories about someone's grandparent or great-grandparent coming through the portal were ubiquitous. Still, I nodded for her to continue.

"I mean, some people deny the Holocaust even happened. Even some Jews, and that was six million people exterminated. 'Well, the walls aren't stained purple. That means this facility did not employ Zyclon-B gas,'" she said, lowering her voice and speaking in a gruff simulacrum of a male authority figure. "So, on one hand, certainly, the thing with the window could have happened: two thousand people fleeing through a rip in the fabric of space. From hell to salvation. Anyone who says differently, well, maybe *they're* the ones reaching. The same sort of people who suggest that the Holocaust never even happened because something they expected to be there wasn't. Or someone *said* it wasn't. Whatever. Our town meeting minutes from back then are chock full of talk about how to feed and care for and even hide the Jews who came over."

I bit my lip as if chewing on her words. "I think I get it. Some people have an incentive to say it happened, and other people will always say it didn't. That it couldn't. But we're not far removed from that time. Refugees who came through are still alive." I dug into my mental list of townsfolk names. Twenty years ago, it would have been a long list. Now, it had grown short and would soon fall to non-existent.

"Mrs. Hosstetter," she mumbled. "Right?"

"Right. She was just a little girl when the window opened. She's still here today." I grew defensive on behalf of the portal, of the people who'd come through. Before that night, the mayor's wife had been a tour guide treating every town legend as credible. Now she was loading the very gun I'd use to punch holes in Fenster's bread and butter, so I had to let her keep going. But part of me wanted her to stop talking. The part that wanted the legend to hold true. I took another drink of my beer and leaned back, trying to ease off so she'd continue. My natural wonder combatting my instincts as a journalist.

She sucked a giant breath and pulled in her lips, making a popping sound when she opened her mouth. "I'm a convert, as you know. When I was a little girl, I lived on a ranch in Texas. My Catholic grandmother raised me; a cruel woman who once force-fed me an entire can of cold and slimy mushrooms because I complained about a shiitake in my salad." She drank deeply from a fresh cocktail, as if washing down the lingering memory. I hadn't noticed the barkeep bringing it over. She moved in close but focused her gaze behind me.

"But she could be kind, loving even. She called me a princess and told me about all the adventures my pony and I would get into. At bedtime she'd reminisce about how Secret and I had chased off the wolves that were killing our sheep. How we rode out into a torrential rain to find a lost foal, not returning till the next morning. How we worked together and baled the basement when it filled with frogs and pond water during a flood. These were amazing stories that came to life in my head. I carried them with me always. I told them to anyone who would listen."

I nodded. "Okay."

"It wasn't until years later when I was in college and met Eli that I reminded my grandmother about those stories. She was sick more and more, and I thought bringing them up would make her feel better. They came to mind as easily as my own name. I could see me and Secret having those adventures as clear as any memory, even when I couldn't remember what I had for breakfast the day before."

She turned to me, and her smile vanished. "And then Granny told me it was all bullshit. None of it ever happened. And she laughed, cackled so hard that she started to hack up phlegm. Even held up a hand like she wanted it to stop. It was too much comedy for her old body to bear." She straightened in her chair, tightened her lips, and took a shallow sip. "I never told anyone that. About it all being a lie. Not even Eli. Every time he brings it up to people, talking about how awesome a childhood I had, I just smile and nod. I can't bring myself to tell him."

After a long silence I said, "And you think that's the deal with Mrs. Hosstetter? That she knows the truth and can't face it?"

She shook her head in tight little motions, but then her smile returned. The cheery smile I had grown to expect over the past weeks. "Maybe she doesn't know the truth. It could be the other way around. At some point, her mother or grandmother considered telling her how they *really* came to America, but they couldn't bring themselves to do it. Maybe they figured it would have been too shameful for her to bear. And maybe it *would* have been. Here she's told scores of tourists and reporters that she passed through the window with a couple thousand others just like her. Imagine if she had to deal with finding out it was all a lie. That would be like calling her life a lie, wouldn't it? Worse than finding out everything you loved about your shitty childhood was make-believe."

A tear escaped each eye and fell down her cheeks, which seemed to surprise her. She pulled back as if raindrops had soaked through the ceiling and landed on her face. She wiped the wetness away with celerity.

I've seen lots of people act out a lot of roles in my career as a journalist, most of which are transparent. She was tipsy and had probably meant to hide behind smiles and fake laughs. Or it could have been a ploy. Something to spin my moral compass and force me to consider what my story could do to Fenster and the people in it.

A glass mug smashed on the other side of the bar, the pieces skittering along the tile floor to a chorus of "oohs." The mayor's wife seemed to wake from a spell, blinking several times in quick succession. "My goodness," she said, her light tone returning. "I think this Cosmo is filling my mouth full of nonsense. I'm sorry to have wasted your time with my ramblings." She laughed like I'd told a joke. The whole time her eyes surveyed me.

I smiled and chuckled along with her, matching her fabricated levity. She had, after all, just given me the most intriguing answer regarding the portal that I'd received over the last month. Something about the entire thing kind of disappointed me, but now I had her and all of Fenster fairly well cornered.

So, I got to feeling pretty smug. I had an ending to my story, straight from the mouth of the mayor's wife. So, when the mayor himself came into the dining area brandishing a quart bottle of German brew, I ordered another round.

Eli Wessel was a ginger-haired, jovial sort. He wore outfits to complement Fenster's German influence: forest greens and high tube socks and even the occasional lederhosen. He kept long sideburns that looked attached with spirit gum for a stage play. He shared the name with many local Jews. Eli rhymes with "belly," which several people reminded me means "uplifted," as in lifted out of Nazi Germany. Over the past month, I'd seen him keying an accordion, drinking a huge mug of dark beer, smoking a curved pipe, a Robin Hood-style hat on his head. Not all at once, but still. I figured he'd added these accoutrements for my benefit when I'd first arrived. I assumed he would eventually break character and show up in sandals and shorts. He never did.

"I hope my wife isn't bending your ear too much," he said, putting his hands on her shoulders and leaning down to our level.

"Well, that's what he's here for, dear," his wife said, patting his hand. "But I'll leave you to continue without me. I've already gone over my two-drink limit and will pay for it in the morning." She rose, hailed the barman, and then pointed to the mayor. The bartender smiled and waved it off, as if her money were no good there anyway.

So, the mayor sat, and we continued. We were two drinks further in—doing little more than rehashing things we had already discussed—when I mentioned what his wife had said. About the portal being convenient. I figured I might goad him into digging a hole alongside hers. Spice up the final sentences even more.

But he stayed silent and drained the last of his beer. He pointed to my glass. "Drink up, Bradley. I want to show you something."

I knocked back my drink, though I'd passed 'soothing buzz' and had wandered into drunkenness. I was grinning by the time we walked outside, the cool evening a welcome change from the day's heat, even into winter.

The mayor led me toward town center, where a stone spire five feet tall marked the portal's alleged location, according to town records. Many disputed the exact spot. No surprise given the many yarns handed down from father to son and mother to daughter since the town's inception fifteen decades ago. The portal had opened a handful of times over that span, they said. Each time someone's great-great-grandfather was the first to go in or the first to greet the visitors from the German side.

He put his elbow on the spire as if placing it atop the shoulder of a friend and then pivoted to face me. He tried kicking up a foot to cross one leg over the other, but he stumbled and barely recovered. "You take a look at that spot, my friend," he said. He pointed behind him with a thumb. "It's magic may not come often, but it is as clear in this town as if a meteor had smashed into us."

I laughed good-naturedly, throwing up my hands. "A meteor filled with German beer recipes and wood-burned signs."

He seemed to ponder this for a moment, maybe weighing whether to be offended, but then belly-laughed. "That's right, Bradley. But you get the idea. If there was no meteor, what else could have done it?" He patted the spire, making a slapping sound that stuck in my head.

Everybody knew that Fenster, Arizona was founded by Germans in the nineteenth century, and local legend said they came not by wagon but through the portal. Which explains why the town looks like they lifted it right out of a "How to be German" handbook—from the signs to the buildings to the roads. But consider what that meant on *their* side.

Think back to the war. That the Jews came through wasn't the mystery. If you assume the portal exists, you would expect an oppressed, hell, *hunted* people to use it for escape. The odd thing was that more didn't come through. The portal opened for a week, long enough for word to get out and for almost two thousand Jews to cross over.

If such a thing happened today, we'd like to think the media coverage would act as irrefutable proof. But even back then they had radio and photography. I saw a photo crowded with people clad in layers of clothes and laden with bags, wearing their babies like backpacks, standing in the middle of the desert, and *I* remained skeptical. We see what we want to see. If the same thing occurred now, if a couple thousand Syrian refugees came through a portal that led to—whatever—some town in Illinois. Say a teenager with quick wits and a cell phone got the whole thing on film and uploaded it to YouTube. A half hour later you'd have people denying its validity.

But say a *million* Jews had come through. The portal would have become something we accepted. Like the aurora borealis, the Northern Lights, right? People had to have thought explorers were making it all up until enough of them saw it or offered ample proof. Now we accept it and study it and all the wonder is gone.

Think about it—how could you hide the fate of a million souls? It stopped after just two thousand escaped because a local named Jon Harper went the other way, from the desert into war-torn Germany. Supposedly the gate shuts as quickly as it opens if someone goes backward. So it's a one-way valve. It doesn't matter which direction you start out; if you renege and go back, it seals up neat as a zipper in the air. Pretty clear now why the Germans settled there. They didn't have a choice. A few of them wander through and then the first one to go back to fetch his wife or grab a torch or whatever, and zip, it's closed again. Hell, it probably opened several times over a few hundred years before they even got *that* right.

I knew all of this; I had spoken to a dozen people in Fenster who corroborated that one notion: don't go backward. One way only.

But it gets sketchy here. I walked past him, the mayor. I wanted to stand in the spot where the portal had opened during World War II and supposedly for a whole month back in the late 1800s. The mayor had encouraged me to do this when I first arrived, but I indulged the urge to do so again.

I suddenly felt colder. If I hadn't been drinking, I might have noticed right away. The desert gets chilly. Fenster sits a thousand feet higher than Phoenix. But this was a wetter, deeper cold. The wind blew from up the street down into the city center, so I turned toward it. I saw the same brick and wood buildings in the yellow light of the streetlamps as I had come to expect.

But different somehow. The buildings seemed dirtier, older. More rounded corners, more imperfections in the stone. I know nothing about biology, but moss clung to their façades like I'd never seen in the desert before. Same with the cobblestone street. It felt like I'd been looking through a filter the last month, and this was the *real* city. I stepped a pace or two. My muscle memory testified to the road's roughness, like I'd been walking on smoother stones these last weeks.

Then I noticed the streetlamps. They gave Fenster—the Fenster in the desert—a sort of charm. I had asked about them the first night, and the mayor said they were electric. The bulbs tapered at the top to simulate the rise of a thin flame. But now the lights burned gas, the flames stoic and still, fire instead of filament. They gave off a low hiss, an oddly comforting sound I would have noticed long before had it always been there.

I looked back at the mayor. He stood open-mouthed, speechless for the first time in four weeks. The sky around him shone a deep blue—would have been black if not for the streetlamps. But it was darker than the surrounding air, extending in a circle to his left and right. It enclosed him, just as a lighter hue must have enclosed me from his point of view.

I smoked for ten years, like every other journalist back before you couldn't even brandish a butt in any public forum. So I knew the scent well, and the air carried a trace of it. Fenster, Arizona was non-smoking except for a single wooden deck at the rear of the inn, closed off and downwind from me. And this was no whiff of a smoker close by, but a lingering miasma. The smell had permeated the stone, the plants and wood.

The street lay empty, but then I heard muffled conversation from inside a building. Laughter is universal but following that laugh came a quick spate of phrases. I might not have gleaned specific words, but the gutturals and umlauts of German were obvious. Sure, some people in Fenster, Arizona speak German. Whether passed down by relatives after traversing the portal or nursed through Rosetta Stone to impress the tourists. But I know well-spoken language, and this came fluid and easy.

"Mayor?" I said through the window. As distant as I felt, I expected my words to fall short. But Mayor Wessel heard me. He looked right into my eyes when I hailed him, then he leaned over and retched into the street. The sound was muffled, like the voices from inside the buildings, though the wet splash and grunting noise of his heaving only traveled ten feet in the night air. Maybe I'm a poor judge of how puking should sound to a drunk man, but it stuck out.

After months of reflecting on that night, I'm not sure the mayor had had that much to drink. More likely the portal opening did it. His whole life he'd banked on its assumed existence. In the faith people put in it. And then there it sat in front of his face. It must have terrified him. An actual rift between thousands of miles that he'd treated as the *fait accompli* of that town, and yet its reality was more than he could process. Or at least *that* night and with the man who would write about it for the whole world to read.

So, as I watched the mayor heaving onto the stone street, my baser nature took hold. Or maybe my subconscious was scared I'd get stuck on the other side, ten feet and five thousand miles away from home, without so much as a passport. Either way, I ran back to the mayor. My ears popped as I passed through the portal and that was that.

He looked up at me like I was a specter come to take him to the afterlife. His face mixed with fear and awe. His mouth hung open, and his bottom lip quivered.

Then he seemed to realize what that meant. He pulled at my shirt and yanked me to the side to peer past me, into the night air. I followed his gaze but saw nothing but the clean streets of the desert Fenster.

"What have you done?" he growled at me. His teeth were clenched so hard I don't think the Jaws of Life could have opened them.

"I'm sorry. I didn't…" I wanted to tell him it was an accident, but the only thing rising in my throat was stomach acid, burning all the way.

"You've ruined us." He sang the words as a terrible wail. "You've ruined me."

I waited for some reveal, like the entire affair had been an orchestrated prank and the townsfolk would pop out in a hail of streamers and laughter. Immediately, I doubted what had happened. I needed to convince myself I hadn't just squandered an event that took place once in a lifetime.

I left Fenster the next morning to little fanfare. No doubt word had traveled about the portal. The townspeople seemed to share the mayor's disappointment. I had let it close without saying hello to a German witness, snapping a single picture, or even staying long enough to convince *myself* of what happened.

I'm telling you now because my story never ran in *American Skeptic*. Sure, the people of Fenster know my name, and so do you, and so does the editor of *Skeptic* if someone really wanted to find me. But I doubt anyone cares that much. I'm not trying to step on your toes. I'm sure you're an able journalist, and that your magazine is respectable, but Fenster is a hard sell *with* reams of proof. Fenster with one more anecdote is no more potent than any other story they tell on the tour. I wish I could speak with a little more certainty, but we'll leave that for the next generation.

I'm sure those couple thousand Jews thought the whole world would be in awe of the miracle that saved them. That we'd stand in horror at the accidental act that doomed so many thousands more. Yet a couple generations later and it's rumor. Hearsay. My story won't even make it that far, but you're welcome to tell it.

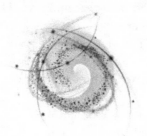

ABOUT THE AUTHOR

Darren is a freelance book editor for Evolved Publications, and his short fiction has appeared in more than thirty publications over the years, including *Hellbound Books*, *Chilling Tales for Dark Nights*, and *The Stoneslide Corrective*. He has had four plays and a feature-length film produced and a non-fiction book published.

While some of his works fall under the literary umbrella, he often returns to genre. His style and reading preferences tend toward the psychological, as he enjoys stories that linger in the imagination long after he's closed the book on them.

He lives in Asheville, North Carolina with his son and girlfriend. See what he's up to darrentodd.net.

MERVIN'S WAND

BY
JAMES RUMPEL

MERVIN'S WAND

The disheveled man blocking the alley was not going to let Karl pass without some sort of interaction.

"Hey, buddy," said the old man, "do you have a few bucks you can spare. I need to eat." His breath reeked of cheap wine.

Karl could have explained that he had no money to spare. He was on his way to see Big Al in order to try and work out some sort of deal to settle a gambling debt. Karl owed Al a lot of money. The one hundred twenty dollars in his pocket was not nearly enough to cover the amount. Instead, Karl just shook his head.

He tried to circle and get into the alley, but the man mirrored his movement.

"How about if I sell you something?"

"What could you possibly have that I would want?" asked Karl. The bum had shoulder-length dirty, gray hair and a long beard of the same hue. He wore a threadbare wool coat that came all the way down to his ankles. A pair of tattered boots covered the man's feet. One of the boots was wrapped in so much duct tape that it was hard to determine if there was any boot left at all.

The old man smiled, displaying half a mouthful of crooked, yellow teeth. "You'd be surprised," he said. "I might not look like it now, but I was once a wealthy man back in England."

"Sure, you were," said Karl. He glanced at his watch. He had to get rid of this fellow quickly. It would not be smart to be late for a meeting with Big Al.

"I was. I was curator of the Arthurian Museum on Portobello Road until I got into some trouble and was run out. I showed them though. I managed to take a few items with me. I've only got one left. I bet a smart guy like you could figure out a way to use it to your advantage. It's magic from the time of King Arthur."

He reached inside his coat and pulled out a wooden wand, holding it up for Karl to see. It was about a foot long and looked like any run-of-the-mill branch except for the odd writing etched into its base and six silver circles running along one side.

"Old man," said Karl, "I'm not going to give you any money for a stupid stick."

"This is not just a stick. It's one of Mervin's wands."

Karl chuckled. "You mean Merlin, don't you?"

"No. Mervin was Merlin's younger brother. He wasn't nearly as powerful or famous as Merlin, but he could still do magic."

"I've heard enough," said Karl. He began to force his way past the vagrant.

"You don't believe me, huh? Well, watch this." The homeless man aimed the wand at Karl and pressed his index finger down on one of the circles.

For a split second, Karl stopped, expecting a fireball or lightning bolt to explode out of the end of the wand. Nothing like that happened. Instead, Karl winked at the old man.

"See, I told you it was magic."

"What?"

"The wand, it made you wink. I admit it's not exactly Gandalf level stuff, but it is magic."

"Okay, I admit that I don't know why I winked," said Karl. "Maybe the wand did make me do it. But, even if it did, you have to admit that isn't very impressive magic."

"Mervin wasn't a very impressive magician. The wand does more than that though. Each of these six circles casts a different spell."

Karl checked his watch again. Maybe it would be worth it to hear the old man out. The money he had wasn't going to cover what he owed Al but maybe he could talk the mobster into taking a somewhat magic wand.

"What else does it do?"

"Well, if you hold the wand like this..." The bum wrapped his pinky and thumb around the base and reached for the second silver circle with his index finger. "...and push this circle you can stop time for everyone and everything except you..."

"Now, that does sound powerful," interrupted Karl.

"...for one second."

"That's all? One measly second."

"Well, it's actually about one and a half seconds. Unfortunately, that's all the longer it works. Remember this is Mervin we're talking about."

"Still," said Karl, "I suppose if you kept doing it over and over you could make use of that spell."

"Except, it only works once per day. Each spell can only be used once per day by the wand's owner."

"That's useless," scoffed Karl.

"Hey, don't blame me. Blame Mervin."

"What do the other spells do?"

"I don't know if I want to tell you. You're probably just going to ridicule the magic anyhow."

"Okay, I'm sorry. Just tell me what the buttons do. There might be something useful."

A smile returned to the old man's face. "There might be. The third one turns one glass of any alcoholic beverage into water. The fourth summons a fly. The fifth makes whoever it targets say the word 'yes' one time. The last one is the best."

"What does it do?" asked Karl, hopefully.

"It can make one character disappear from anything written in ink."

"So, it's a really bad eraser."

"A magical really bad eraser."

Karl looked at the wand and shook his head. "So, none of its spells actually do anything. Why would I want it?"

"There is one more thing. Legend has it that if the owner is worthy the wand brings them good luck."

"It doesn't seem to have brought you much luck," laughed Karl.

The old man shrugged. "Maybe I'm not worthy."

"I'll tell you what. I have to admit you've been interesting to talk to even if your wand is totally useless. I'll give you a dollar for it."

"That's insulting," said the old man. "This wand has been useless since the days of King Arthur. Make it fifty."

"Five."

"Twenty-five."

"I won't give you more than ten."

"Twenty and your belt."

"Fifteen"

"Just twenty. You can keep your belt."

"Deal."

Karl had his hands behind his back as if he were standing at attention. He stood like that as a gesture of submission to Big Al, but also because it allowed him to hold the wand without Al seeing it. Karl didn't know when or how he was going to offer the magic item, but he wanted to be ready when the moment came.

Al sat at a table in the back of his bar, The Broken Knuckle. Two beefy thugs flanked him. They both stared at Karl with narrow eyes and blank expressions.

"I believe you're a bit behind on your payment schedule," said Al. He started to page through a notebook.

Karl wasn't sure why he did it. Maybe he just wanted to make Big Al suffer the tiniest bit of aggravation. Maybe his subconscious had come up with a plan. Whatever the reason, Karl discretely directed the wand at Al and pushed a circle.

Almost immediately, a fly began buzzing around Al's face. Momentarily forgetting about looking up Karl's debt, Al frantically waved his hands at the insect.

"You, stupid bug," shouted Al while he took a swing at the fly. The mobster's hand knocked into a glass of beer, toppling it. "Damn." He scrambled to prevent the papers on the table from getting soaked. "Tony. Go get a rag and bring me another beer," he ordered.

The bodyguard to his right immediately took off toward the bar. Al sat with the notebook in his hands, waited for the table to be cleaned before continuing to look for the amount of Karl's debt.

When Al's minion returned, he handed the beer to his boss and began wiping the table.

Karl couldn't help himself. He pushed another button on the wand.

Al took a sip of his fresh beer and immediately spit it out. "What the hell? I told you to bring me a beer, not water, you imbecile."

"I did bring you a beer," stammered Tony.

"Don't you lie to me," shouted Al. "Do you think I'm stupid?"

Karl pushed another circle.

"Yes," said Tony. Instantly, his eyes widened, and he gasped loudly. "I mean, no. Of course not."

Al's face was beginning to turn the color of a strawberry. "Are you telling me you brought me water by mistake?"

232

Tony nodded vigorously. "Yes. That's it. It was a simple mistake. I would never do anything to disrespect you."

Tony winked.

"Why you…" shouted Al, his face now the color of a ripe tomato. He turned to his other bodyguard. "Rocky. Teach this punk a lesson."

Without a word. Rocky took a swing at Tony. His fist flying above Big Al's head. At least it started over Al's head.

Karl activated the wand again. In the little over a second that he had while everyone was frozen in time, he leaped forward and pulled Rocky's fist down a couple of feet. He jumped back as the bodyguard completed his swing, landing it squarely on Big Al's nose.

The scene that followed was pure chaos. Al, Tony, and Rocky went at each other as if they were in a professional wrestling battle royale. Punches were thrown, chairs shattered, tables overturned. Al dropped his notebook and tackled Rocky. Tony jumped on top of both of them.

Karl took advantage of the diversion. While the mobsters were busy beating each other's brains out, he grabbed the notebook and flipped to the page with his name on it. He took his wand and pushed the sixth and final button. Miraculously, the final zero on the 'amount owed' line simply disappeared. Karl dropped the book and backed as far away from the combatants as possible.

Soon, a half dozen more of Al's men charged into the bar. They pulled Rocky and Tony off of Al and escorted them out the back door. Karl didn't want to think about what was going to happen to them.

Four bodyguards remained. They helped Al up and reset his table and chair. Slightly bruised and still the color of an apple, Al took a deep breath. He looked up and saw Karl standing in the corner.

"You. Come here right now."

Karl obeyed.

"First off, don't you tell anyone what you just saw. Do you understand?"

Karl nodded.

"Good. Now, about your debt. I'm in no mood to compromise. If you don't have the money that you owe me, you are going to be very sorry." He turned a couple of pages in the notebook and stopped. He stared at the page in front of him. "I guess you only owe one hundred dollars. I thought it was more. Whatever. I've got other things to worry about. Pay up now, or else."

Karl smiled as he reached into his pocket and pulled out his money. He set it on the table and left without another word.

On his way home, he looked for the old man who had sold him the wand but could not find him anywhere. *"That's too bad,"* he thought, *"I wanted to tell him that Mervin wasn't that bad of magician after all."*

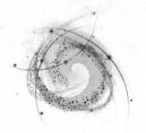

ABOUT THE AUTHOR

James Rumpel is a retired high school math teacher who has greatly enjoyed spending his additional free time trying to turn some of the many odd ideas circling his brain into stories. He lives in Wisconsin with his wonderful wife, Mary.

WORRY DOLLS

BY
CARLA WARD

WORRY DOLLS

Late in the afternoon, Loretta Silverman approached her
daughter's doorstep, clutching the handle of a small blue gift bag.
Her stomach churned with both excitement and dread. She was
eager to see her grandson, Liam, but her daughter, Erin, not so
much.

When she knocked on the front door of the shabby home, white
paint curls sloughed off and floated toward her sandals like snow.
But unlike real snowflakes, they didn't melt as they landed on the
sunbaked porch.

Moments later, Erin appeared in the doorway, wearing short
shorts and a tight yellow tank top, a cigarette pinched between two
red acrylic nails. "You should've called first. I don't like when you
just stop by." Though well into adulthood, she still sounded like an
insolent teenager.

From the day Erin freed herself from Loretta's womb, the girl
had been difficult. A colicky baby, she screamed and fussed non-
stop the first year of her life, fraying Loretta's nerves like unraveled
yarn. Around eighteen months, as the colic subsided, the tantrums
began and never stopped. Twenty-six years later, Erin still hadn't
learned to behave.

"Sorry. I forgot," Loretta said, though she wasn't one bit sorry.
If she had called beforehand, she would've been told to stay home.

Seven-year-old Liam sidled up beside his mother and smiled at
Loretta, his brown eyes glittering with curiosity. "Hi, Grandma!" He
rushed onto the porch to hug her, then pointed at the gift bag in her
hand. "What's that?"

"A little something for you."

Erin scowled. "What's the occasion?"

"No occasion." At least, none that she could mention. She was
here because of Liam's recent visit with the school psychologist, a
subject Erin refused to discuss, because according to her, nothing
was wrong with the boy. He just needed to toughen up.

Liam glanced back at his mother. "Can I open it?"

She flicked the ash from her cigarette onto the porch. "I guess."

Loretta handed the bag to her grandson.

He peeled away the tissue paper and peered inside. "What are these?"

Erin stepped forward and looked over Liam's shoulder. "Yeah. What *are* those?"

"They're worry dolls."

Liam reached into the gift bag and pulled out one of the five little figures resting at the bottom. Inspecting it closely, he admired the embroidered eyes and mouth and ran his fingers over the traditional dress, sewn from colorful textile scraps.

He glanced up at his grandmother. "Why are they called worry dolls?"

"They're supposed to help you stop worrying. I read they work wonders for children who have—" Loretta nearly blurted out *anxiety*, Liam's official diagnosis, but caught herself. "—have a lot of fears."

"Did you sew them yourself?" Erin wrinkled her nose. "They look homemade."

Loretta shook off the insult. "They are. The website I bought them from said they were handcrafted in a Guatemalan village."

Erin smirked, shaking her head. "Thanks for giving my kid toys from a third-world country."

Liam put the doll back in the bag and selected another. "How do they work?"

"Before you go to bed, you tell them about your worries," Loretta explained. "Then you put them under your pillow, and they do your worrying for you while you sleep."

According to the charming legend outlined on the website, the dolls would also remedy the *source* of one's anxiety, but she didn't mention that. She didn't want him thinking the dolls were magic genies rather than what they were—surrogate counselors. Erin had made it clear Liam wouldn't be going to any sort of therapy, so Loretta bought the dolls, hoping they would help him cope with his anxious thoughts.

"Okay, visiting time is over," Erin announced.

"Thanks, Grandma," Liam called as his mother hauled him by the arm back into the house.

"You're welcome."

Liam disappeared, and Loretta was left alone with her daughter.

"Next time, call first." Erin puffed on her cigarette, then exhaled smoke in her mother's face. "Got it?"

Loretta waved her hand, gagging on the taste of ashes. "I was just trying to help."

"You wanna help? Try getting out of my business." Erin stepped inside and slammed the door, making Loretta flinch.

Erin's lack of respect was nothing new, but today it was easier to let it go. Loretta had accomplished her mission: deliver her gift to Liam. That was all that mattered.

Later that evening, Liam leaned his head under the faucet of the bathroom sink and slurped enough water to rinse the toothpaste from his mouth. After he swished and spat, he dried his face on a hand towel and enjoyed the minty tingle on his tongue.

He often wished Erin were more like his friend Henry's mom, who always smelled Henry's breath before bedtime to verify his chompers were clean. Erin never even asked if Liam had brushed his teeth, let alone checked. He worried her lack of interest meant she didn't love him.

As he stepped out of the bathroom and padded down the hall toward his room, he noticed his parent's bedroom door was ajar. Moving closer, his mom came into view. She stood beside her bed, packing a suitcase that sat on top of the mattress.

He crept closer and nudged the door open a little further. "Where are you going?"

"Out of town. I'm leaving after I drop you off at school tomorrow."

"Who's gonna take care of me?" He prayed she'd say Grandma Loretta.

"Your dad. *For once.*" She muttered the last bit.

His dad never watched him. He was always too busy working overtime at the grocery store.

"How long will you be gone?"

"Just one night." She stopped packing long enough to look at him, annoyance etched into her pretty face. "Don't give me the puppy eyes. I deserve to go out. Being your mom is hard, you know."

Invisible pins pricked the backs of his eyes. He didn't understand why she needed to go somewhere overnight. She went out with her friends all the time, leaving him home alone for five or six-hour stretches. He never complained. It hurt the way she talked about him, like he'd worn her out. If he had, he hadn't meant to.

"Who will paint the customers' fingernails while you're gone?" He was only seven, but he knew how important jobs were to grownups. His parents often griped about how hard it was to pay the rent on their little house. Maybe by making her worry about her job at the nail salon, he could convince her to stay.

"I traded my shift with someone. They're more than enough girls to take care of things." She shut the lid of the suitcase and yanked the zipper around the sides. "Go to bed."

It crossed his mind to ask her to tuck him in, but he thought better of it. The only time she was willing to do that was when she'd had a few glasses of her special ice tea, the kind made by a guy named Jim Beam. Only then could she be persuaded to help Liam to bed and turn off his light, but those times were rare. Not the tea drinking, that happened almost every evening, but her slipping into a motherly mood didn't.

"Good night," he murmured and plodded back across the hall to his room.

After he closed his door, he turned off the light and crawled into bed next to the five worry dolls lying on his pillow. In the glow of the night-light—the one Grandma Loretta had given him because he was afraid of the dark—he gathered the dolls and squeezed them to his chest.

"I'm supposed to tell you my worries, huh?" He blew out a long breath. "Well, I worry about this boy in my class, Ryker." Just saying the kid's name aloud made Liam shudder. "A few days ago, he kneed me in the privates." The memory conjured a faint wave of nausea. "He got suspended for a day, but when he came back, he told me that next time, he'd hurt me worse, when no grown-ups were around." He squinched his eyes shut. "So, I'm worried about what he'll do to me next."

Hugging the dolls tight, he imagined the little hand-stitched figures absorbing his fear like a sponge. Within seconds, the heaviness in his chest lifted and was replaced by a calming warmth.

"Thanks for listening," he told the dolls as he slid them under his pillow. "It helped."

He fell asleep almost instantly, something that hadn't happened in years.

Erin squeezed the steering wheel, frustrated with the jerk-off in front of her. The guy was going exactly thirty, which *was* the posted limit, but there weren't any cops around. Didn't he know you were supposed to go five over?

It never failed. Whenever she was running late, she got stuck behind some old geezer. She reached for her pack of smokes sitting in the cup holder, popped one out, and lit it. After a couple drags, her nerves settled.

"What time will you get back tomorrow?" Liam spoke in that mopey tone she hated. He had an instinct for making her feel guilty.

"I don't know." She sucked hard on the cigarette filter. No matter how pathetic the kid sounded, she wouldn't reconsider going away with Brad for a night.

Unlike her husband Dwayne, Brad was in shape and knew what he was doing in bed. The last few weeks, she and Brad had been screwing in the unholiest of places, including the bathroom of the bar where they first met and the storage closet at the nail salon where she worked. Tonight, they were staying at a motel. Nothing fancy, but there'd be a mattress under her head, and she wouldn't have to stand up for a change.

Liam sniffled, but she ignored it. The kid cried over everything. If she acknowledged his tears, he'd cry even harder. She kept her eyes on the road. Soon, she would divorce Dwayne and make him take custody of Liam. Then she'd be rid of them both.

When she pulled up to Liam's school and parked at the curb, the boy didn't move. Just sat there in his seat, hunched over.

"Hurry up, kid." His dark eyes found hers, and her heart clenched. How could he make her feel like complete shit with just one glance? "Liam Anthony Draper, get out of this car."

"Don't go tonight," he murmured.

She leaned across his lap and pulled the passenger door handle. The door swung open. "Go."

Liam slowly put his backpack on. "Have fun on your trip."

"Oh, I will."

After Liam shut the door, she pulled away from the curb, happier than she'd been in months.

When the dismissal bell rang, Liam followed his classmates as they filed out of the building. Lined up on the sidewalk, the children waited for their respective rides to arrive. After standing in the heat for twenty minutes, all the other first graders had left with their loved ones, leaving Liam alone with his teacher, Mrs. Meyer.

Liam worried his dad had gotten lost. After all, he'd never been to Winslow Creek Elementary before. Driving Liam to and from school was his mom's responsibility.

Mrs. Meyer took his hand and said in that sweet voice of hers, "Let's go inside and give your folks a call."

Just as they turned to leave, his dad's ancient Honda Civic roared through the parking lot and stopped at the curb a few feet in front of them.

"Here he is."

"That's your dad?"

Liam nodded.

"*Oh.*"

There was something in that one syllable that told him Mrs. Meyer didn't like his dad. Maybe because Dwayne's car had a crooked fender and a rash of rust that made it impossible to tell what color it used to be. Or maybe it was the cigarette hanging from his bottom lip. Polite ladies like Mrs. Meyer didn't like things like that.

Liam released her hand. "Bye."

Concern pinched the corners of her mouth. "Have a nice weekend."

He got in the car and buckled his seatbelt. "You were supposed to come at three-thirty."

"Don't talk to me like that." Dwayne shifted gears and punched the gas. The sudden lurch whipped Liam's head back against the seat. "You're lucky I'm here at all."

"Sorry."

"You *are* sorry." Dwayne nursed the tip of his cigarette, then spewed a gray cloud. "A sorry excuse for a male."

As they drove away, Liam stared out his window, trying to recapture the happiness he'd felt at school. Today had been the kind of day he would've written about had he owned a diary. He still couldn't believe his good luck.

Ryker was gone.

At first, he'd assumed his tormentor was out sick, but then Mrs. Meyer informed the class that Ryker had moved out of state over the weekend. In a blink, all Liam's worries about being hurt again vanished. It was a miracle.

"Listen," Dwayne said, interrupting the boy's thoughts. "I know I'm 'watching' you." He made air quotes with the hand clutching a cigarette. "But I'm going to uh . . . I've got a meeting tonight."

"Grocery stores have meetings?"

"Shut your yap. The point is, I won't get home until after midnight. I'll put a sandwich in the fridge for your dinner."

Liam nodded, unable to utter the frightening questions now racing through his mind. *What if a stranger knocks on the front door? What if I choke while eating my sandwich? What if I get sick?* There was no point in asking. His dad would just give him that irritated look and say, *Don't be such a pansy.*

Leaning back in his seat, Liam watched the world whiz by in a blur, wondering how he would get through tonight. Then he got an idea. "Since you'll be gone, can I go over to Henry's and hang out?" Henry was a classmate whose house was six blocks from Liam's.

"Sure." Dwayne tossed his smoldering butt out the window. "But be home before dark."

"Could you give me a ride there?" Liam knew he was pressing his luck, but his fear of walking there alone outweighed his fear of his father's ridicule. Absorbing a few insults was worth it if he could avoid facing The Beast.

The Beast was a mean pit bull Liam encountered each time he ventured to Henry's. Because the sidewalk only ran on the side of the street where the dog lived, Liam didn't have a way of getting around it. Not unless he walked in the street, which he wasn't supposed to do.

The massive dog lived in somebody's backyard, tethered to a metal stake. Whenever the boy walked past, the dog would charge toward him until the rope tied to its collar ran out of slack, putting it within a few feet of the buckled sidewalk. The last time Liam faced The Beast, it pulled so hard on its rope the stake loosened a little, giving the hellhound a few extra inches of reach. It hadn't escaped, but Liam had gotten a close-up of The Beast's teeth. The image of those yellow fangs still haunted him.

"Don't be lazy, numbnuts." Dwayne maneuvered the car onto their street and past several tiny homes like theirs, all in need of repair and fresh paint. "You can walk."

Sadness flooded the boy's chest, drowning his heart in a pool of black hopelessness. He had two options. Stay home and be driven crazy by his fear of being alone or make the nerve-racking trek to Henry's.

He opened his backpack and grabbed one of the worry dolls he'd taken with him to school. "I'm worried the dog will eat me," he whispered in its ear.

"What the hell is that?"

"Nothing." Liam chucked the colorful figure into the dark mouth of his bag and zipped it shut.

"Was that a *doll?*" His dad pulled into their driveway and killed the engine. "Since when do you play with dolls?"

"I—I don't." His heart crashed against his ribs. His dad believed boys should play football and baseball, not with dolls. If Dwayne knew about Grandma Loretta's gift, he might take them away. "It's a project we made at school."

"Glad my hard-earned taxes are paying for your arts and crafts." His dad sounded annoyed, but not at him.

Liam exhaled a long, relieved breath.

"You can go to Henry's. But make sure you're in bed by nine." Dwayne squinted like he meant business. "I expect you to be asleep when I get home. If you're not, your ass and my belt will have an appointment, understand?"

The boy nodded. "Yes, sir."

Liam slipped into the straps of his backpack and started down the cracked sidewalk that would eventually lead to Henry's house. Taking small, deliberate steps, he delayed the confrontation with The Beast for as long as possible. Thirty minutes later, he approached The Beast's fenceless, grassless yard. The lot was full of dog turds but oddly, no dog.

A familiar bark rang out behind him. He turned around slowly, petrified to face The Beast, but he wasn't there. Nothing was there except an ambulance-like vehicle parked at the nearby curb with

ANIMAL CONTROL in big blue letters on the back. Then it dawned on him. The dog was inside the vehicle's cargo.

Liam's relief was so intense his knees nearly gave out.

"You okay there?"

The male voice startled him. He hadn't noticed the man in a tan shirt and shorts standing next to the vehicle.

"I'm fine, sir," Liam said. "You're taking the dog that lives here?"

The man dabbed his sweaty brow with the back of his hand. "Yep. I have to. He's not being fed and watered. The owner's been neglecting him."

Inside the vehicle, The Beast let out a whine, like he was sad to be reminded.

"Will he find a new home?" Liam asked, feeling a little sorry for the dog now that he understood his owner hadn't taken care of him.

"Hopefully, yeah." The man fished his keys from his pocket. "Look, I gotta go, kiddo."

Liam waved and watched him drive off. When he'd recovered from his shock, he continued to Henry's, skipping all the way.

Saturday morning, just as Loretta was pouring a cup of coffee, her cell phone rang. When she saw her daughter's name on the display, she couldn't help but groan. Erin never called unless she wanted something. Usually money.

Loretta accepted the call, put the phone to her ear, and forced herself to sound pleasant. "Good morning, Erin."

"Hey, I need two hundred bucks. I'm short this week."

Loretta rolled her lips inward and clamped them between her teeth, the only effective way to keep her opinions to herself. Her daughter had a habit of going out with friends, running up an outrageous bar tab, and then using her grocery money to cover it.

"Short, huh?" Despite Loretta's best efforts, disdain bled into her voice.

"It's not like I don't work." Erin sounded defensive. "Sometimes there's not much left after paying the bills."

"You mean your entertainment expenses?"

"Do you want your grandson to eat this week or not?"

That stuck Loretta right between the ribs. As much as she wanted to argue, she didn't want to risk her grandson going hungry. "Of course, I do." She rubbed her temple where pressure was building into an ache. "I'll go to an ATM and get it for you. When should I bring it by?"

"Oh, no you don't. We're not turning this into a visit. I'll meet you at the ATM."

Loretta frowned. So much for that. "How about the one on Locust Street?"

"Fine, but I have to work today, so it'll need to be in half an hour."

"Alright." Loretta hesitated, then asked, "If I can't see my grandson, could I at least say hello to him?"

Erin let out an exasperated huff. "I'll give you two minutes. Here he is."

"Grandma?"

The boy's voice soothed her tried patience. "Hi, Liam. How are you?"

"Um, okay, I guess."

"Is your mom standing right there?"

"No, she's in her room getting some medicine. Her trip gave her a headache."

Loretta rolled her eyes. Sounded like Erin was hungover. "Her trip?"

"She went somewhere, overnight, but I don't know where."

Loretta had long suspected Erin and Dwayne were no longer faithful to each other. She wondered if her daughter had gone somewhere with a lover. As much as she wanted to satisfy her curiosity, she knew better than to grill Liam for more details. If Erin caught him telling tales out of school, she might ban him from speaking to his grandmother forever.

"So, did you and your dad have fun last night?" Loretta asked, changing the subject.

There was a long pause. "I hung out with Henry, then came home and went to bed. Me and Dad didn't have time to do anything."

Something in the boy's tone told her he wasn't being entirely truthful, but she decided not to press it.

"How are the worry dolls working out?"

"They're great. They make my worries go away."

"So, talking to them makes you feel better?"

"Yeah, but that's not what I meant. They actually fix your problems."

"How so?"

"Well, there was a kid at school who liked to hurt me, but after I told the dolls about him, he moved to another state. And when I told them I was afraid of the scary dog who lives up the block, he was taken away by an animal controller."

Loretta recalled the legend associated with the worry dolls. Maybe experiences like Liam's helped perpetuate belief in the folklore. "I can see why you think it's the dolls, but it's not. There's a word for this—*coincidence*. Do you know what that is?"

"No."

"It's when two things happen at the same time, but neither of them has anything to do with the other. It's all an accident, not on purpose."

"This seemed on purpose to me."

"I'm sure it did but—"

"Time to get off," Erin boomed in the background.

"Bye, Grandma. I love—"

A tone beeped in Loretta's ear, indicating the call had ended. She chuckled bitterly. Paying a hundred dollars a minute to speak to her grandson, she thought Erin could have allowed her a proper goodbye. But Erin only cared about one person in this life—herself.

Sunday evening, just before midnight, Liam woke to his parents' shouting. In the silvery glow of his night-light, he sat up in bed and listened. It was hard to make out everything, but snippets came through clearly enough. His dad yelling w*hore*. His mom shrieking something about *screwing all the checkout girls*.

Pressing his hands to his ears, he tried to block out their hateful words, but it didn't work. He could still hear their loud, angry voices. Sinking under his covers, he pulled the worn comforter over his head and dug the worry dolls out from under his pillow. He hugged them to his chest.

This wasn't his parents' first argument. They fought a lot, almost every time they were in the same room, but this particular fight had a sharper edge to it.

I want a divorce. His mom's shrill voice penetrated his blankets. He wondered if he'd heard right. Never before had the D-word come up.

Lots of kids in his class had parents who were divorced, so he knew what it meant. Divorce was when you lived with your mom on school days and visited your dad on the weekends. Maybe he would too, and life would be better.

For just a moment, the idea comforted him, but the more he imagined it, the more he realized a divorce couldn't solve his problems. He was sure his parents would still fight, even if they didn't live together. It was as if they *enjoyed* yelling and arguing, were drawn to it the way they were drawn to cigarettes and Jim's ice tea.

The yelling grew louder and louder until it ended with a crash, like glass shattering against a wall. *We're through.* His mom that time. Then stomping in the hall and the slam of the front door.

Liam squeezed the dolls tighter. "I worry they'll never stop fighting."

A sense of peace washed over him as if he'd slipped into a bath of warm water. He slid the dolls under his pillow, then drifted back to sleep.

Monday morning, Liam was finishing a math test when the school secretary's voice crackled through the intercom, interrupting the silence.

"Mrs. Meyer, could you send Liam Draper to the office, please?"

"Of course." Mrs. Meyer glanced over at Liam. "Just turn your paper over before you go."

He did as he was asked and slowly made his way to the office, worried he was in trouble.

When he arrived at the secretary's desk, she greeted him with a strange, flat smile that said she felt sorry for him. His stomach got all queasy. Judging from her expression, an awful fate awaited him.

"Liam," she said gently, "someone is here to see you." She pointed to the hallway that led to the principal's office, a place he'd never personally visited but had heard about. He trudged in that direction. When two plastic chairs just outside the principal's door came into view, he saw Grandma Loretta sitting in one of them.

Forgetting the rule about running indoors, he dashed headlong into her arms. She swallowed him in a hug and squeezed him longer than she usually did. When she finally released him, she studied his face like it was a riddle she was trying to solve.

"What's the matter?" he asked.

Her blue eyes were watery. She looked tired and sad. "I'm afraid I have some bad news." She stopped a moment, swallowed so loud he heard a faint *click*, then she continued in a trembly voice. "Something happened to your parents."

Whatever it was must've been terrible, or Grandma Loretta wouldn't have visited him at school. "What happened?"

"A car accident." She sniffled. "They didn't survive."

He blinked. His parents were dead?

He thought back to last night when he told the worry dolls about his mom and dad. Goose pimples erupted on his arms, and a shiver rippled through him. He hadn't meant to get them killed.

Then he remembered Ryker and The Beast. *They* hadn't died. They were just sent elsewhere. Maybe the worry dolls didn't have another way to make his parents stop arguing.

Tears trailed down Loretta's face, but Liam couldn't summon any of his own. He scraped the bottom of his heart for memories of his parents, acts of kindness they'd shown, anything that would make him miss them, but sadly, found none.

He wiped his grandma's cheeks. "I'm sorry I can't cry."

"Don't apologize." She kissed his forehead and pulled him to her. "You're in shock, honey. It's perfectly normal."

He relished the comfort of her hug, the sense of safety it gave him. They held each other for what seemed like a long time. Then a question came to mind.

Lifting his head, he asked, "Why were they in the same car, Grandma? They didn't go anywhere together."

"They, uh, were on their way to the courthouse."

He wondered if the courthouse was where people got divorced, but he didn't bother asking. A more urgent question needed answering. "Where will I live now?"

"With me." She tilted her head. "If that's alright with you."

His heart swelled with happiness, like an overfilled water balloon, ready to burst. The idea of waking up in a home that was always quiet, always calm, and living with a person who would never hurt you seemed too good to be true.

His vision blurred with hot tears. "I'd like that."

"Good." Loretta kissed the boy's cheek. "Now, go get your bookbag. You're leaving early today. We have a lot of arrangements to make."

"Okay." He gave her one more squeeze, then hurried out of the office and back to the first-grade hallway. As he opened his locker, his classmates filed out of Mrs. Meyer's room, heading toward the double doors that led to the playground.

Emma, the redhead whose desk was next to Liam's, watched him get his backpack. "You leaving?"

"Yeah." He noticed she was wearing long sleeves again, even though it was way too hot for clothes like that. But after what happened last week, he knew why she was covering her arms.

They'd been sitting side by side on the swings, catching their breath after playing tag. She didn't know he was looking when she pushed up a sleeve to peek at the bruises just below her elbow. He figured someone in her life must've been a lot like his dad.

"Hey, Emma, I want to give you something." He pulled the five worry dolls from his bag and handed them to her. "I think you need these more than I do."

She examined them closely, touching their stitched faces. "What are they?"

"Worry dolls."

ABOUT THE AUTHOR

Carla Ward has published over a dozen short stories in various genres: mystery, romance, literary, and low fantasy. If she's not at the keyboard, you'll find her taking long walks or reading the latest Dean Koontz book.

Her work has appeared in *Night Picnic*, *Laurus*, *Oakwood Magazine*, and *Woman's World Magazine*.

https://twitter.com/Carla_Ward_
https://www.instagram.com/carla.ward.author/

THE MYSTICAL ROCK

BY
PEGGY GERBER

THE MYSTICAL ROCK

Annie shrieked as she hit the ground with a thud. She had been running for the bus when she tripped on an object, soared a foot into the air and fell down hard. Her floral skirt billowed around her head as she moaned, "Just my luck."

Nothing in Annie's life had been going well lately. She hated her job, nobody would publish her book, and, after two years of trying, she still wasn't pregnant. She had a history of depression and now she felt it creeping back in, and she didn't have the energy to do anything about it. The only good thing she had in her life right now was her husband Jacob, and their relationship had been strained lately due to all the tension in the house.

Annie's face flushed crimson as she sat on the ground and began to assess her injuries. She had fallen very hard on her hands and expected one or both of her wrists to be broken. The last time she fell like this she was in a cast for six weeks. Annie began flexing her wrists and examining her knees for injuries and wondering why she wasn't in pain. Other than ripped pantyhose, a couple of light scratches on her hands, and a bruised ego, she felt completely fine. She stood up slowly and began searching for the object that tripped her. When she looked down, she spotted a rock the size of a grape, smooth and black, with a beautiful, intricately designed Hamsa painted on it. She picked it up and examined it with a feeling of awe growing inside of her. The ornamental hand was painted a rich blue color with delicate swirls of purple and specs of gold glitter. She thought the rock was one of the most beautiful pieces of art she had ever seen.

Annie knew exactly what the Hamsa symbol meant because her mother often wore a Hamsa necklace for good luck. She owned one in every color and size. She believed the Hamsa symbol represented the hand of God and would ward off the evil eye. She was always trying to get Annie to wear one. She said it might help her with her struggles. Annie always groaned at her mother and told her to leave her alone. Unlike her mother, Annie was not superstitious. But there was no denying there was something special about the rock. Annie carefully wiped off all the dirt, placed it in her pocket, and continued on to work. As she got closer it briefly crossed her mind that perhaps it was the rock that saved her from harm. She then shook her head and laughed at herself.

Annie tiptoed into her office an hour late, still flexing her wrists, and prepared herself for the inevitable lecture from her boss. As she walked in her friend Kristy jumped up to meet her with a big grin on her face and said, "Today's your lucky day Annie. Mr. Jenkins called and said he was having car trouble. He will not be in until the afternoon."

Annie sighed with relief and did a little happy dance as she settled into her workstation. All morning long she kept sneaking peaks at the beautiful rock and wondering about it.

When it was time for lunch, Kristy met Annie at her desk, and they walked to the cafeteria together. As Annie described her eventful morning, she pulled the rock out of her pocket and placed it in Kristy's hands exclaiming, "Isn't this the most gorgeous Hamsa you've ever seen? The artist is amazing. I don't know how anyone could have painted such an intricate design on such a small rock."

Kristy rolled the rock back and forth in her hands and said, "Annie, I'm bewildered, it just looks like a plain, black rock."

Annie frowned. "Kristy, that's not funny. You are making me sound crazy, and you know I am sensitive about that."

Kristy gently placed her hands on Annie's shoulders and replied, "I would never make fun of you. I swear, all I see is a black rock."

At the lunch table, Annie passed the rock around to her co-workers and asked what they saw. They all agreed there was nothing special about the rock and asked Annie if she was feeling okay. Kristy tried to make Annie feel better by suggesting that perhaps the rock was like that dress that was posted a Facebook a couple of years back. Although most people saw the dress as blue, some saw it as gold.

After a very confusing day Annie walked home from the bus wondering if she was having hallucinations. She figured either her luck was about to change, or she was becoming unhinged. As she walked past the local convenience store, she impulsively went inside and bought a lottery ticket, immediately pulling out a coin to scratch off the numbers. She pumped her fist into the air when she realized she had won fifty dollars. It was the first time she had ever won anything, and she celebrated by picking up Chinese food for dinner.

When Annie arrived home, she put the food in the oven and turned on her computer to check her email. Her heart began to pound when she saw she had mail from an agent, and her breath caught as she clicked it open. Her breathing became even more ragged as she read the message.

The agent loved Annie's book and wanted to represent her. Her book would be published. Tears began flowing down Annie's face as she re-read the email five more times.

As soon as Jacob walked through the door, Annie jumped into his arms and began sobbing. She asked him to pinch her to make sure she wasn't dreaming. After telling him all about her weird, wonderful day, she tentatively put the rock in his hand and asked what he saw. She closed her eyes and hoped he saw the same thing as she did.

He shook his head and said, "Annie, all I see is a black rock, but I really do believe you, and I've always believed in you. I am so happy for your good news."

The next day, Annie bought a special little acrylic box to keep the rock in and carried it with her wherever she went. Her luck continued to grow, and she soon began getting acceptances for many of her previously rejected short stories. Six months later she was posing for the camera as she proudly held her first published novel in her hands. When her book began to get good reviews, it gave her the confidence she needed to quit her job and become a full-time author. The ideas for her next book were flowing freely, and her old writer's block was a thing of the past. Every morning now Annie woke up with a smile on her face, and without her even realizing it, her depression had faded away. Annie felt genuinely happy.

It was about a year after finding the rock that Annie and Jacob made plans to meet at their favorite restaurant to celebrate their anniversary. Annie arrived first and was seated near the window by the hostess. Soon after, Jacob walked in carrying a dozen roses, and Annie's face lit up when she spotted him.

As he joined her at the table, he took her hands in his and said, "Annie, we have had such a wonderful year. I am so proud of you and how well your new career is going. I love you so much. Let's go crazy and order the most expensive bottle of champagne in the restaurant."

Annie replied, "Thanks honey, I love you too, but I will not be drinking for at least another seven months."

They made a toast to their wonderful news with a bottle of grape juice and discussed all the events of the past year. Annie said, "Jacob, I owe everything to my good luck rock. It completely changed my life. My book got published, I haven't felt depressed in a very long time, and the best news of all, we are expecting a baby. How else could you explain it, it had to be the rock."

"Annie," Jacob said, "you sent query letters to like a thousand agents, and your book is wonderful. You are a very talented writer. I always said sooner or later some agent is going to be smart enough to represent you. That's not luck, that's hard work and talent."

Annie furrowed her brows. "Well, how do you explain my depression getting better? I had been feeling awful for such a long time."

"Annie, you went to a therapist for a year. You practice meditation, you write in a gratitude journal, and you've worked so hard doing all the exercises your therapist gave you. You need to give yourself credit for feeling better."

Annie sighed. "Okay Jacob, here's the biggest thing, I have been trying to get pregnant for two years now, and it's finally happened. How do you explain that? It has to be due to the luck of the rock, doesn't it?"

"Honey," Jacob said, "you had been so stressed for such a long time. You are finally relaxed now. Maybe your body was smart enough to know that now is the right time to have a baby."

On the ride home, Annie thought about everything Jacob had said. It made a lot of sense, but there was still one huge unanswered question. Why was she the only one who could see the Hamsa on the rock? That had to mean something, didn't it?

A week after their anniversary dinner, Annie and Jacob went to the radiology center for her first ultrasound. As usual, Annie had the rock in her purse and touched it for reassurance while they awaited their turn. As Annie looked around the office, she noticed a little girl of around five years old sitting on her mother's lap clutching a pink teddy bear.

The little girl appeared sickly and was resting her head on her mother's shoulder. Annie looked at the little girl's mother and saw there were tears in her eyes.

Annie impulsively jumped up and approached the little girl saying, "Hi, my name is Annie, what's yours?"

The little girl smiled, "Hi, my name is Jasmine, and this is my teddy bear. Her name is Jasmine too."

Jasmine's mom looked up and smiled at Annie, grateful for the distraction.

Annie continued, "Jasmine, do you want to see something super cool?"

Jasmine beamed. "Yeah, I want to see something super cool!"

Annie put the rock in Jasmine's fragile hand and asked, "What do you see?"

Jasmine's face lit up as she said, "Mommy, look at the beautiful orange butterfly. It's just like the one we saw at the park last week. Isn't it so pretty Mommy? Can I keep it Annie, can I?"

Annie turned to Jasmine's mom and asked, "Can you see the butterfly as well?"

She contorted her face. "Of course."

Annie could not see the butterfly, and to her amazement, could no longer see the Hamsa. All Annie could see was a plain black rock. Now she knew for sure this rock was meant for Jasmine.

She told Jasmine's mother, "This rock will bring you good luck, but you must promise to take good care of it. I don't understand why or how it works, it just does. Bring it with you to all of Jasmine's doctor's appointments."

Although Jasmine's mom appeared skeptical, she and Jasmine promised to take good care of it, and Annie walked away with a spring in her step.

Annie smiled at Jacob as she took his hand and followed the technician to the ultrasound room. They waved good-bye to Jasmine, who was busy showing the butterfly to Jasmine the Bear. Annie told Jacob, "I just knew the rock was meant for her. I'm ready to make my own luck now."

A year later, as baby Felicity was taking a nap in her crib, Annie began work on her newest novel. She already had a title for it: *The Mystical Rock*.

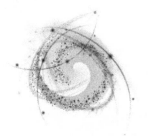

ABOUT THE AUTHOR

Peggy Gerber is the 2021 winner of the Open Contract Challenge and author of the poetry chapbook, *Stumbling in CrazyTown*. When she is not writing poetry, Peggy likes to indulge her love of speculative fiction by writing stories of time machines, aliens and creepy dolls.

Her work has appeared in many publications including *Daily Science Fiction*, *The World of Myth Magazine*, *Everyday Fiction* and many others. Peggy lives with her husband in New Jersey and enjoys reading, traveling and playing with her grandchildren.

ADDITIONAL COPYRIGHT INFORMATION

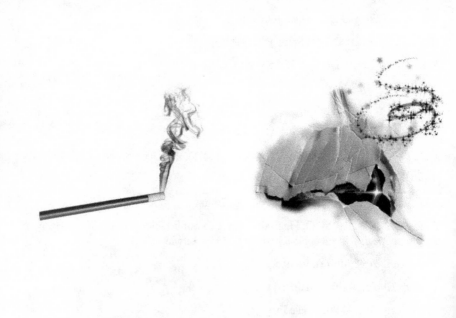

Printed in the USA
CPSIA information can be obtained
at www.ICGtesting.com
JSHW082310250124
55961JS00001B/25